Remarkable

★ A novel by ☆

Lizzie K. Foley

Dial Books for Young Readers

An imprint of Penguin Group (USA) Inc.

Dial Books for Young Readers

A division of Penguin Young Readers Group • Published by the Penguin Group
Penguin Group (USA) Inc., 375 Hudson Street, New York, New York 10014, U.S.A.
Penguin Group (Canada), 90 Eglinton Avenue East, Suite 700, Toronto, Ontario, Canada
M4P 2Y3 (a division of Pearson Penguin Canada Inc.) • Penguin Books Ltd, 80 Strand,
London WC2R 0RL, England • Penguin Ireland, 25 St Stephen's Green, Dublin 2, Ireland
(a division of Penguin Books Ltd) • Penguin Group (Australia), 250 Camberwell Road,
Camberwell, Victoria 3124, Australia (a division of Pearson Australia Group Pty Ltd)
Penguin Books India Pvt Ltd, 11 Community Centre, Panchsheel Park, New Delhi—110 017,
India • Penguin Group (NZ), 67 Apollo Drive, Rosedale, Auckland 0632, New Zealand (a
division of Pearson New Zealand Ltd.) • Penguin Books (South Africa) (Pty) Ltd, 24 Sturdee
Avenue, Rosebank, Johannesburg 2196, South Africa • Penguin Books Ltd, Registered
Offices: 80 Strand, London WC2R 0RL, England

This book is a work of fiction. Names, characters, places, and incidents are either the product
of the author's imagination or are used fictitiously, and any resemblance to actual persons,
living or dead, business establishments, events, or locales is entirely coincidental.

The publisher does not have any control over and does not assume any
responsibility for author or third-party websites or their content.

Library of Congress Cataloging-in-Publication Data
Foley, Lizzie K.
Remarkable : a novel / by Lizzie K. Foley.   p. cm.
Summary: Ten-year-old Jane Doe, the only student average enough to be excluded from
the own of Remarkable's School for the Remarkably Gifted, is joined at her public school
by the trouble-making Grimlet twins, who lead her on a series of adventures involving an
out-of-control science fair project, a pirate captain on the run from a mutinous crew, a lonely
dentist, and a newly constructed bell tower that endangers Remarkable's most beloved
inhabitant—a skittish lake monster named Lucky.
ISBN 978-0-8037-3706-8 (hardcover)
[1. Eccentrics and eccentricities—Fiction. 2. Ability—Fiction. 3. Secrets—Fiction.
4. Pirates—Fiction. 5. Community life—Fiction. 6. Humorous stories.] I. Title.
PZ7.F7316Re 2012   [Fic]—dc23   2011021641

Published in the United States by Dial Books for Young Readers,
a division of Penguin Young Readers Group
345 Hudson Street, New York, New York 10014
www.penguin.com/youngreaders

Designed by Jennifer Kelly
Printed in USA

1 3 5 7 9 10 8 6 4 2

TO JON and DASH—
the two most Remarkable guys in my universe

A Remarkable Town

High on the top of a majestic mountain, in a spot where every view of the valley below was more breathtaking than the next, was a small town called Remarkable.

The town had not always had this name. It once had been called something rather ordinary, like Hoopersville, or Hill Valley, or some other name that no one could remember anymore. But whenever tourists came to visit, they couldn't help but notice what a remarkably nice place it was. The air was always fresh and the weather was always pleasant. The parks smelled like newly cut grass, and unlike most local museums, the Museum of Remarkability wasn't the least bit dusty or dull. There was a beautiful lake known as Lake Remarkable, and nearby were three elegant glass-domed buildings that housed the world's largest live butterfly collection. Additionally, Remarkable was home to the world's two tallest trees, a celebrated science fair, and the best organic jelly that anyone had ever tasted.

As you might expect, the people who lived in Remarkable were pretty splendid, too. They tended to be terribly interesting and even more terribly talented. In fact, they were among the most terribly interesting and talented people in the whole wide world. The tourists felt lucky just to breathe the same sweet air as all of these important individuals, and the important individuals thought the tourists were lucky, too.

Long after the tourists went back to their drab little lives in the drab little places they had come from (and their friends and coworkers had grown sick and tired of hearing about their vacations) they just couldn't seem to stop talking about how the town they had visited had been remarkable—Remarkable. Eventually, the town was called Remarkable so often that this became its name.

But this is not to say that everything in Remarkable was remarkable. It had a very dull post office, for instance, and it had a Coffeebucks that sold coffee that was very good, but certainly no better than the coffee served at any other Coffeebucks in any other town. And then there was Jane, who was a very unremarkable girl, ten years old, of medium height, with eyes of no particular color, and hair that was not quite brown enough to be called mousy.

There was no reason that Jane should have been so unremarkable. She was the daughter of astoundingly brilliant parents. Her mother, Angelina Mona Linda Doe, was a famous architect who had designed the many spectacular buildings in Remarkable's terrifically charming downtown. Her father, Anderson Brigby Bright Doe II, was an award-winning novelist whose thought-provoking books (and striking cleft chin) were discussed in depth at book groups all across the country. When they decided to start a family, everyone in town figured that their children would be geniuses. And everyone would have been right, too, if it were not for Jane.

Jane had an older brother named Anderson Brigby Bright Doe III. He was remarkably good-looking—so handsome, in fact, that people often stopped him in the streets to tell him about it. These comments always made him blush right to the roots of his wonderfully wavy hair, giving everyone the impression that he was also quite modest—which made him seem even more handsome, since modesty is an attractive quality.

Besides being good-looking, Anderson Brigby Bright Doe III could paint pictures with such precision that they looked just like photographs. His parents were so proud of him that they couldn't wait to have another child. Two years and two days after Anderson Brigby Bright Doe III was born, Jane entered the world, although hardly anyone noticed.

Now all babies are beautiful, but some babies are less beautiful than others, and then there are some babies who are just beautifully plain. Jane's parents had intended to name their daughter Penelope Hope Adelaide Catalina, but when they looked at her face for the first time, they realized that the name would not do at all. She was the plain kind of baby, maybe the plainest baby anyone had ever seen, and much too plain to have a long and fancy name. After a hushed discussion, they named her Jane instead.

They saved the name Penelope Hope Adelaide Catalina for Jane's younger sister, who was born two years and two days after Jane. Penelope Hope was an adorably cute child with a wonderfully practical mind.

She also happened to be a genius at math. Once, when she was just six years old, the cash register broke at Mr. Filbert's fine grocery store, so she'd been asked to spend an entire afternoon adding up all of the customers' purchases in her head. She also went over Mr. Filbert's taxes and found that he was owed a great deal of refund money from the government—enough, in fact, that he was finally able to afford to send his two children to Remarkable's School for the Remarkably Gifted. Mr. Filbert offered Penelope Hope a giant lollipop as a thank you, but Penelope Hope was as sensible as she was good at math, and she asked if she might have a nice healthy apple instead.

It was a sad day for Jane when Mr. Filbert's children, Antonia Annabelle and her brother, Humphrey Douglas Filbert, were enrolled in Remarkable's School for the Remarkably Gifted. It meant that she was the only student in the entire town left at the regular public school. Her brother and sister had been going to the gifted school ever since preschool, but her parents had never bothered to send Jane there, because there wasn't any reason to.

So now Jane sat alone in the middle seat in the middle row of the fifth-grade classroom where every desk was empty except for hers. She had no one to push in the swing at recess, no one to eat lunch with, and no one to serve the volleyball to in gym class. Given that she was the only student in the whole school, she should have at least gotten a lot of attention from the teachers. Unfortunately, this was not the case. As often as not, the teachers forgot she was there at all and spent the entire day drinking coffee and playing fantasy football in the teachers' lounge.

Penelope Hope was sure Jane must be lonely, and because she was as kindhearted as she was good at math, she tried to help.

"Maybe," she told Jane, "you could convince Mom and Dad that you're gifted at being unremarkable. Maybe they'd let you go to the gifted school then."

It wasn't a bad idea, but Jane knew it wouldn't work. She might be unremarkable, but compared to her grandfather John, she wasn't even all that remarkable at being unremarkable. Her grandfather was the most unremarkable man in the world. He was so unremarkable that people were always introducing themselves to him like they'd never met before, even though he'd lived in the town for years and years. Then they'd immediately have to ask him his name again because they would have forgotten what he had just told them.

Of course, it didn't really matter that Jane's grandfather was easy to forget, because Jane's grandmother was memorable enough for both of them. Grandmama Julietta Augustina was Remarkable's mayor and had lived in Remarkable longer than anyone else. In fact, she'd been there so long that she'd started taking the town's remarkableness for granted. As a result, she was remarkably hard to impress. She nearly always snorted "hmph!" disapprovingly whenever anyone tried to show off for her. Of course, this meant that every talented person in Remarkable was desperate to get her approval, and she could hardly go anywhere without having someone try to astound or amaze her.

Grandmama Julietta Augustina was always very nice to Jane, partly because Jane never tried to impress her, and if she was disappointed that her granddaughter had no special talents, she never let anyone know about it.

"I'm glad you're you, Jane," she'd say, unless she was having one of her distracted days, in which case she might temporarily forget Jane's name and have to call her "honey" or "sweetheart" until she remembered it again.

The Grimlet Twins

On Friday afternoons after Jane got out of public school, her grandfather would take her to Mrs. Peabody's Colossal Ice Cream Palace, which served the best ice cream in the whole world. It was supposed to be a special treat—but it never wound up being very special, because they never actually got any ice cream.

Every week, Grandpa John ordered two medium-sized vanilla sundaes with no chocolate sauce, no whipped cream, and no cherry on top. And every week, Mrs. Peabody forgot to bring their order to them. Mrs. Peabody didn't blame herself for this. It wasn't her fault that Jane and Grandpa John were so much less memorable than all of her other customers.

But on this Friday, while they were waiting in vain for Mrs. Peabody to notice them, a straw wrapper suddenly came flying out of nowhere and struck Grandpa John in the middle of the forehead.

Now, Jane knew that someone had deliberately blown the straw wrapper, but she didn't for a second think that whoever it was had meant to hit her grandfather. Grandpa John had probably just been in the way of whomever the straw-wrapper shooter had intended to hit.

But then the most remarkable thing happened. Another straw wrapper came gliding through the air and struck Grandpa John above the left eyebrow. When a third straw wrapper hit him, this time a little lower and right between the eyes, Jane had to consider the possibility—impossible though it seemed—that someone was deliberately targeting her grandfather.

She turned around and saw that the wicked Grimlet twins were sitting behind her. They had a big stack of wrapped straws on their table, and they were peeling the ends so they could blow the wrappers off. The Grimlet twins were new to town, and they came from a notorious family. Mr. and Mrs. Grimlet were rumored to have robbed a bank before moving to

Remarkable, and no one had been able to prove that the rumor wasn't true.

Jane didn't know what to do. If she'd been Anderson Brigby Bright Doe III, she would have marched right over and told them to stop. He was so handsome that people always did what he asked. If she'd been Penelope Hope Adelaide Catalina, she probably would have gotten her own pile of straws and engaged the Grimlet twins in a wrapper-shooting battle, which they were sure to lose because Penelope Hope Adelaide Catalina had deadly aim. But since she was just Jane—and there wasn't anything she was particularly good at—she chose to do nothing at all.

The Grimlet twins were identical, which was surprising considering that Eddie Grimlet was a boy and Melissa Grimlet was a girl. They both had short blond hair, squinty eyes, and runny noses that were covered in dirt and freckles. Neither one of them smiled very often, unless they were smiling about getting away with something nefarious.

Jane waved shyly at one of the twins, and he or she grinned back. The other twin shot a straw wrapper at her, and it hit Jane squarely on the tip of her very plain nose.

* * * * *

The Grimlet twins were long gone from the Colossal Ice Cream Palace by the time Jane and her grandfather came to their usual sad conclusion that they might just as well give up on Mrs. Peabody and go home hungry. But Grandpa John was still craving something sweet, and so he gave Jane a dollar and asked if she would mind going to Wembly's Superior Drugstore to buy him a packet of figgy doodles. Then he sat down on a bench in the park across the street to wait for her.

It was an errand that should have only taken a minute. Grandpa John liked a plain, mostly tasteless kind of figgy doodle that came in an old-fashioned paper wrapper. Mr. Wembly kept them on a bottom shelf at the back of the store because no one else ever wanted them.

As she walked past the pet supply aisle, Jane couldn't help slowing to look at the many fine products Mr. Wembly had for sale. She wished she had a reason to buy a fancy beaded dog collar, or a box of all-natural dog chews. Jane loved dogs and suspected that she'd discover she was a highly talented dog owner if her parents ever remembered to let her get one.

When Jane paused to admire a particularly fluffy cashmere dog sweater, the Grimlet twins came around the corner as they stampeded toward the drugstore's exit. And since Jane wasn't the sort of person that other people notice when they are stampeding, the Grimlet twins ran right into her.

WHOMP!

The Grimlets had just purchased five hundred gum balls, eighteen bottles of bluing rinse, and fifty-four boxes of mousetraps. The gum balls shot all over the floor; the mousetraps started snapping away in their boxes; and the bottles spun and skidded in every which direction. One of the bottles broke and made a big blue puddle on Mr. Wembly's freshly mopped floor.

The Grimlet twins stared at Jane, surprised to find her at their feet.

"So sorry," one of them said, not sounding sorry at all. "We didn't see you."

"Which is strange when I think about it," the other one said, "since we've been following you for days."

"You've been following me?" Jane asked, hastily getting to her feet. The big blue puddle was spreading toward her sneakers. "What for?"

"Because you're the girl who goes to the public

school," replied the Grimlet twin standing closest to Jane.

"So very fortunate for you," said the Grimlet twin standing farthest from Jane.

"What do you mean by fortunate?" Jane asked. She was sure that the Grimlet twins were making fun of her somehow, but their wicked faces were oddly earnest.

"It seems like a fascinating place," said the first Grimlet twin. "I hear the food in the cafeteria is dreadfully ordinary."

"And I hear," said the other one, "that you can get into trouble for all kinds of things—like passing notes, and copying homework, and talking in class."

"I suppose that's true," said Jane, even though she didn't know this for a fact, since there was no one in the school for her to talk to, copy homework off of, or pass notes with. "Don't you get in trouble for that at the School for the Remarkably Gifted?"

The Grimlet twins shook their heads sadly.

"I'm afraid not. We've tried many times, but the gifted teachers know we're just trying to develop our talents for rule-breaking, so they encourage us to try harder."

"That doesn't sound so bad," Jane said. But the Grimlets once again shook their heads.

"There's not much point in causing trouble if nobody minds."

Just then, Mr. Wembly, the pharmacist who ran the drugstore, came running over to see what had happened. "I thought I told you two not to come back here!" Mr. Wembly shouted at the Grimlet twins. "Now clean this up and get out!"

He was an unpleasantly uptight man who hated noise and mess. Unfortunately, Jane's accident with the Grimlet twins had produced a remarkable amount of both.

"Don't mind him," one of the twins told Jane. "He's still angry at us for setting off his burglar alarm last week."

"I'm sure you didn't mean to," Jane said.

"And I'm sure we did. We adore loud noises," the other twin said.

The Grimlet twins began the grim task of picking up nearly everything they'd dropped in their collision—except for the broken bottle, which they kicked under the cosmetic counter with the hope that Mr. Wembly wouldn't notice, and the puddle of bluing rinse, which they left on the ground with the hope that someone would slip on it. They staggered under the weight of their purchases, and Jane could see that they were in danger of dropping everything again.

"Wait!" Jane called after them, "I could help you carry some of that if you want."

"We'd appreciate it, of course," one Grimlet said. "But you'd risk being implicated as our accomplice."

Jane wasn't sure what "implicate" or "accomplice" meant exactly, but she took two grocery bags full of mousetraps and followed the Grimlet twins out of the store.

The creepy black house where the Grimlet twins lived was not far away. Normally it should have taken only a few minutes to walk there, but the Grimlets couldn't seem to go more than a few steps without trying to trip each other or knock each other off the sidewalk.

Jane followed along behind, hoping that the Grimlet twins might invite her to come inside when they arrived home. No one ever went into the Grimlets' house, except for the Grimlets themselves, so it would be very exciting to be asked. But exciting things did not happen to Jane, and once they reached the front gate of the creepy black house, the Grimlet twins stopped.

"Thanks for your help," one Grimlet twin said, taking the two bags out of Jane's hands. "But we have to go now. We have to get a very important school project ready for next Wednesday."

"But we'll see you around sometime," said the other. "Sometime soon."

Jane said good-bye and walked dejectedly back down the hill toward home. People were always telling her that they'd see her around, but then they usually forgot to ever notice her again.

That night at the dinner table, Jane's mind was occupied with two things. The first was her brief and wild encounter with the Grimlet twins. The second was a nagging feeling that she'd forgotten something important. She'd had that feeling ever since she'd gotten home.

This wouldn't have been a problem if Jane were more like her mother. Jane's mother never forgot anything. As an architect, she had many important projects and proposals to keep track of, so she kept a planner filled with daily to-do lists, weekly schedules, and monthly timetables to help her keep everything straight. Right now, she was looking over her list of family-related action items.

"How was school today, Jane?" she asked. "Demonstrate interest in Jane's life by asking her about school" was Action Item #27. Other items included "Make sure Anderson Brigby Bright has unplugged his electric paint warmer" (Action Item #16), and "Don't let Penelope Hope eat citrus fruit because she is allergic" (Action Item #22).

Jane shrugged without answering as she served herself some salad. Her mother wasn't interested in the truth, which was that school, as usual, had been very boring. She passed the salad bowl to her brother, who didn't even look up when she set it down in front of him. Anderson Brigby Bright was busy sketching a picture of a girl with chic glasses, a well-shaped nose, and long black braids on his napkin. Her father was staring into space and muttering to himself—something he did when he was thinking about his novel. Jane's mother gave him a nudge and nodded toward Jane to remind him to take an interest in his middle child (Action Item #32).

"Oh, hello, Jane," her father said. It was as if he'd

noticed her at the table for the first time. But Jane didn't take this personally. Her father was deeply absentminded. "Did you enjoy your bagpipe lesson today?"

The bagpipe lessons were a birthday present he'd given her. He'd mistakenly believed that this would be something she would be good at. Sadly, she was even more average at bagpipes than she was at most things. Still, it had been a better present than the one her mom had given her, which was a book entitled *Your Exceptional You-ness, A Preteen's Guide to Discovering Your Hidden Talents, Even When No One Thinks You Have Any.*

"My lesson wasn't today. It was on Tuesday," Jane said.

"Isn't it Tuesday?" He tended to lose track of Tuesdays the same way he lost track of his keys, his umbrella, and the phone bill.

"It's Friday, Dad," Penelope Hope Adelaide Catalina said, looking up from a notebook she'd been filling with quadratic equations.

"Oh. It's Friday! So Grandpa took you out for ice cream after school today, right?"

Jane didn't answer him. She'd suddenly remembered what it was she'd forgotten. "Oh no," she groaned. "Grandpa!" She excused herself from the table and ran back to the park.

There was a slight chill in the air, and it was just starting to get dark by the time Jane reached the bench where she had left her grandfather—but he was still sitting and waiting patiently.

"Oh, Grandpa!" Jane said. "I'm so sorry. I didn't mean to leave you here!"

"It's perfectly all right, my dear." He never minded being forgotten, which somehow made Jane feel even worse. He stood up, moving a little stiffly after sitting for so long.

"I don't suppose you remembered to buy my figgy doodles, did you, Jane?" Grandpa asked as they started walking back to her house together.

"No," Jane said miserably as she realized she still had the dollar he'd given her. "I'm afraid I forgot about them, too."

"It's not important," Grandpa John said. "I think I still have a few left over." He patted his coat pocket, and Jane heard the crinkle of a paper figgy doodle wrapper.

Remarkable was lovely in the dusky evening light. Fireflies hovered in the air. Birds twittered their evening love songs. People were out and about, enjoying the last few moments of the beautiful day before night set in.

As they walked, Jane glanced up at Grandpa John, and wondered—as she often did—if anyone recognized him as the husband of the mayor of Remarkable. She doubted it. Most people were stunned when they realized that Grandmama was married to Grandpa John. They had a hard time imagining how such an incredibly boring man had won the heart of someone as awe-inspiring and dynamic as Julietta Augustina.

The story went like this: When Jane's grandfather was a young man, he decided to learn to juggle. So one day he went to the side of the road with three oranges and started to practice. He soon figured out that juggling with three oranges was practically impossible, so he tried juggling with just two, but that wasn't much less impossible. Finally he settled for juggling just one orange.

Right then, Julietta Augustina came racing past in her high-performance sports car. When she saw the man tossing the orange into the air, she hit the brakes, turned the steering wheel hard with just one hand, and skidded in a perfect U-turn so that her car screeched to a stop in front of him.

Julietta Augustina took off her crash helmet and shook out her long auburn curls. She pulled off her racing goggles and looked at him with eyes that were a blue so electric that the summer sky looked gray in comparison. Then she'd folded her arms and said:

"What are you doing?"

"I'm juggling," he replied.

"Hmph!" she said, snorting just a little as she spoke. "I'm not very impressed."

"So what?" he answered.

Grandmama Julietta Augustina stared at him. She'd never before met anyone who didn't care what she thought. Grandpa John stared back. It was the first time in years that anyone had bothered to ask him what he was doing and then stayed to listen to the answer. And right there, right on that spot on the side of the road, they fell in love. Grandpa John climbed into her sports car, and they drove to Remarkable to get married that very day. It all made perfect sense to Jane. Grandmama and Grandpa were such opposites that it was obvious they belonged together.

When Jane and Grandpa John reached the front steps of her house, he gave her a kiss on the forehead and told her good night.

"Aren't you going home?" Jane asked. Normally, he would have continued past her house and on to the mayor's mansion, which was farther up the road. But today he turned to walk back the way they'd just come.

"I'll head there soon enough," Grandpa John said. "I just have to run a quick errand down at the lake first."

"Oh," Jane said. "Well, I'll see you tomorrow, I guess." Then she went inside and left Grandpa to wander off in the direction of Lake Remarkable by himself.

The Lake Monster Festival

Despite what some people may say, it doesn't take much to put a town on the map. Usually, all a town has to do is exist, and cartographers—the people who draw maps for a living—will mark its location on any map they're making with a small dot. It doesn't matter if the town is so dull that no one wants to know where it is, or so boring that no one would ever want to visit it. Cartographers don't like to leave things out, and they will still put all the boring, dull towns on their maps because that's what cartographers do.

Of course, even cartographers had to admit that a small dot was not enough to do justice to Remarkable. Whenever Remarkable was put on a map, its name was marked by an asterisk as well as a dot, and this asterisk guided the map reader's attention to the lower right-hand corner where there would be an extra box under the map's legend that listed many of Remarkable's finer attributes. This extra box would no doubt mention that a great many of the town's citizens were people who were famous, but it would also have to acknowledge that the town's most famous citizen wasn't a person at all, but rather a serpent named Lucky.

Lucky lived in Lake Remarkable, which was a beautiful lake that was known for its sweet-tasting waters and its large schools of flying fish. Lucky was larger than Nessie, the Loch Ness Monster of Scotland, even if she wasn't as famous. Of course, this was only because Lucky was much more elusive and much too clever to ever allow herself to be photographed. Those few who had been lucky enough to catch a glimpse of Lucky claimed that she was purple and black with a snakelike body, three big humps, and a long snout full of very sharp teeth.

Lucky had been heard more often that she'd been seen. It was said she made a soft calling sound that was somewhere between an eerie *hoot* and a haunting *coo*. In Remarkable, nearly everyone believed that hearing Lucky's call was a sure sign of good luck. Bronson Seurrier claimed to have heard it just as he bought the lottery ticket that won him the mega jackpot for the second time. Elinor Rosalind Wallace heard it just before the Swedish king called to tell her she'd won her third Nobel Prize in Chemistry and one in Physics, too. Even Grandmama had heard it once—on the night before she met Grandpa—and she always said that meeting Grandpa was the luckiest thing that had ever happened to her.

Of course, Lucky's existence wasn't just interesting to those who lived in Remarkable. Many people from outside of Remarkable were interested in her, too. Once a year, the government would send a team of cryptozoologists—who are people who investigate mysterious creatures for a living—to try to capture Lucky so that she could be studied by important scientists.

The cryptozoologists would spend a week hiding in the bushes with tranquilizer guns or rowing around the lake with large fishing nets and blowing on small whistles to try to lure Lucky out into the open. It never worked. Lucky was even more elusive during this week than usual.

When the week was over, and the cryptozoologists had packed up their nets and whistles and gone home, the town would celebrate with its renowned Lucky Day Festival. It was a marvelous event. There were snow cones and cotton candy, free T-shirts, and carnival rides. Every year Jane went with her family, and she enjoyed standing off to one side watching as everyone else in town had a great time.

This year, the town was using the festival to raise money to build a bell-tower addition to the post office to keep it from looking so ordinary. The town had commissioned a thrillingly talented composer named Ysquibel to write a song that would chime every day at noon from the tower's fifty-seven brass bells.

Ysquibel was Europe's most famous composer, who had recently and mysteriously disappeared during a performance of his latest opera, *Prise de Corsaire*. Fortunately, the last thing he did before he vanished was put the sheet music for Remarkable's bell tower in the mail.

Jane's mother was the architect for the new bell tower, and she'd brought a dollhouse-sized model of her design to display on a pedestal near the free T-shirt stand. It was the best architectural model of a post office addition that anyone had ever seen. People kept coming up to Angelina Mona Linda Doe to tell her she'd outdone herself. Even Grandmama Julietta Augustina had been impressed enough to say, "Well, Angelina, it's not completely terrible."

The rest of Jane's family was getting a lot of attention at the festival as well. Jane's father's newest book had just hit the bestseller list, and he was being followed by crowds of people who wanted him to sign their copies. Mr. Phelps, the bank president of Remarkable Savings and Loan, had asked Penelope Hope Adelaide Catalina to explain compound interest to him, and Anderson Brigby Bright III was being giggled at by a bevy of girls from Remarkable's School for the Remarkably Gifted. They all thought he was so cute and so modest, and they were all hoping to get a chance to ask him to the upcoming annual Science Fair Dance.

It was while Jane was standing off to one side watching her family have such a good time that she suddenly had the sensation that someone was staring at her. Now, the sensation of being stared at is always an uncomfortable one, but to Jane it was even more uncomfortable because it was also unfamiliar.

She looked around, half expecting to find the four beady eyes of the Grimlet twins watching her. She winced in anticipation of being hit with a straw wrapper again. But the Grimlets were nowhere to be seen. Perhaps her imagination was running away with her, but this seemed unlikely because her imagination wasn't the kind that did much running.

Then Jane saw someone wave to her. It was Dr. Josephine Christobel Pike, Remarkable's exceptionally proficient dentist. Dr. Pike was making her way to Jane through the crowd while carrying an enormous puff of bright pink cotton candy on a paper cone.

"Hello, Jane," Dr. Pike said. "Are you enjoying the fair?"

"Uh-huh," Jane said, but she was too surprised to say more. Dr. Pike had a small wisp of cotton candy stuck to the corner of her mouth. Such a sugary snack seemed like an odd choice for a dentist, but it wasn't odder than the fact that Dr. Pike knew Jane's name. Dr. Pike only saw Jane twice a year. Usually people needed to see Jane a lot more often than that to remember her.

"I just wanted to remind you that you have an appointment on Tuesday. It's at two thirty," Dr. Pike told her.

"Yes, right . . . umm. I'll be there," Jane stammered.

"Wonderful. I've been looking forward to it for months."

If Jane had been able to read minds, she might have been surprised to discover just how eagerly Dr. Josephine Christobel Pike anticipated her twice-yearly dental appointments. But Jane wasn't the least bit telepathic, and so she had no idea that she was Dr. Pike's favorite patient.

So, instead, Jane was stunned. Dr. Pike had remembered her name, and she was looking forward to seeing her? It was very, very strange.

She looked around to see if anyone in her family had noticed what had happened to her, but of course, no one had. Her mother had pulled out her planner and was showing her grandmother a detailed flow chart of tasks that needed to be completed before the bell tower's groundbreaking ceremony. Her father was still signing copies of his new book. Penelope Hope had finished explaining compound interest to Mr. Phelps and had moved on to helping him understand third-world debt relief, and Anderson Brigby Bright was staring off into the distance at nothing in particular.

Or so it seemed at first. But the more Jane looked

at her brother, the more she recognized that he was staring at a girl.

The girl was humming—and rather loudly, too— as she listened to a small music box that Jane's mother had put in the dollhouse-sized architectural model. The music box played a simple version of Ysquibel's thrilling composition. Every time it stopped, she wound it up again and hummed along as if this was the most important task in the world.

The girl looked familiar, but it took Jane a moment to realize why. She was the same girl that Anderson Brigby Bright had been sketching on his napkin at the dinner table. It would be impossible not to recognize the long black braids, chic glasses, and well-shaped nose from Anderson's photorealistic napkin sketch. The only detail he had missed was a large button pinned to the girl's lapel that read S.Y.N!C.

"Who's that?" Jane asked her brother.

"Her name is Lucinda Wilhelmina Hinojosa," he said wistfully. "She has perfect pitch."

"What's perfect pitch?"

Anderson Brigby Bright didn't answer her, and it occurred to Jane that he was looking at Lucinda Wilhelmina Hinojosa the same way that most of the girls from Remarkable's School for the Remarkably Gifted looked at him.

"Oh," said Jane. "Oh. You like her, don't you?"

Anderson Brigby Bright tore his eyes away from the strange, humming girl long enough to give Jane a mournful look.

"I think I'm in love," he said. "But she doesn't know I exist. Can you imagine anything more awful?"

Jane's imagination didn't have to run away with her at all for her to understand how he felt. It was a feeling she knew all too well.

The Dentist's Lament

Jane was late to her dentist appointment on Tuesday, but this was not her fault.

Her father was supposed to pick her up from school and drive her to Dr. Pike's office. For once, he'd remembered to show up on time (reminding him about important appointments was Action Item #34 on Jane's mother's list), but then he had accidentally locked his keys in the car. So Jane wound up having to walk up the hill to Dr. Pike's office while her father waited in the school's parking lot for one of Remarkable's highly competent automotive locksmiths to open his car door for him.

Jane wanted to explain to Dr. Pike about the locked

car and the long uphill walk, but Dr. Pike—who'd been torturing herself with the thought that Jane wasn't coming after all—was eager to get to work. She hurried Jane into the exam room and began X-raying her mouth.

"So tell me," she asked Jane. "Have you been brushing twice a day?" She was hoping Jane would say no, so she could deliver a nice stern lecture on the importance of oral hygiene. But all Jane said was "Urgurguhuhruf." She had the bitewing tray in her mouth, and she couldn't really talk.

Dr. Pike finished with the X-rays and began examining Jane's teeth. "Hmmm," she murmured. "Open wider." She poked and prodded at Jane's mouth with a periodontal probe and dental mirror. "It looks like you have a teensy bit of plaque and just a hint of tartar . . . but I guess it's not too bad. Have you been flossing regularly?"

"Uhguhguhgugh," Jane said.

"I see," Dr. Pike said. She poked around Jane's mouth some more. She switched her periodontal probe for a dental explorer, and her mirror for a tongue retractor.

Finally, she was done. "Well," she said. "I don't

see any cavities right now. Not even a tiny one. . . ." She sighed despondently, set her dental instruments down on a tray, and handed Jane a cup of water so she could rinse and spit.

"But that's good, right?" Jane asked. She wasn't sure why Dr. Pike seemed so disappointed.

"Well, yes, I suppose so. I mean, of course it is. I was just hoping . . ." Dr. Pike let her thoughts drift. "Well, thank you for coming in. I guess I'll see you in six months? Does that sound okay?"

"Sure," Jane said. "I'll see you then."

As soon as Jane was gone, Dr. Pike grabbed a lollipop from inside her desk and stuck it in her mouth. She knew better than to eat something that was so likely to promote tooth decay, but she couldn't help herself. She was depressed, and she always craved sugary snacks when she was depressed.

Dr. Josephine Christobel Pike was a very good dentist. She could put a filling in a tooth so gently that she didn't even need to use novocaine. She could take dull, yellow teeth and polish them until they were bright and white again. She had a wonderful flair for curing gum disease and gingivitis, and her patented techniques for performing dental extractions and root canals were taught in every dental school in the country.

Dr. Pike had replaced Dr. Bayonet, who'd been the dentist in Remarkable before she arrived. Dr. Bayonet was gruff and grouchy—which was possibly due to the fact that he was much more interested in being an amateur lepidopterologist (who is a person who collects butterflies) than he was in fixing teeth. One day he decided to build the world's largest live butterfly collection—and he'd become so preoccupied with catching specimens for it that he'd quit coming into work. Eventually, Grandmama Julietta Augustina was forced to hire a new dentist. She'd heard that Dr. Pike was the best, and so she asked her if she'd be willing to take over Dr. Bayonet's practice. Dr. Pike was only too happy to accept.

It didn't take Dr. Pike long to discover that if a dentist wanted to look at rows and rows of perfect teeth, then Remarkable was certainly a good place to work. The citizens of Remarkable had remarkably strong teeth, and they knew how to take care of them, too. In the two years that she'd been in Remarkable, Dr. Pike had seen nothing but beautifully white teeth in beautifully wide smiles.

Now, Dr. Josephine Christobel Pike liked beautifully white teeth in beautifully wide smiles as much as the next dentist, but this meant that no one in Remarkable really needed her services. It didn't matter that she knew how to cure all different kinds of gum disease when no one in town ever seemed to suffer from any of them. It didn't matter that she could drill a painless filling when no one ever got a cavity.

The only exception to this was Jane. Jane's teeth weren't terrible—but she did have an average number of cavities for a girl her age, which wasn't very many, but it was enough to remind Dr. Pike how much she liked fixing teeth. And now she wouldn't see Jane again for six months, and Jane might not have any tooth-related woes for her to fix then, either.

In the meantime, all she could hope for was that the Grimlet twins would stop by again to visit her. They were tied for her second favorite patients, but this wasn't because the Grimlets had tooth decay like Jane. Their teeth, although surprisingly sharp, were as white and perfect as everyone else's.

Dr. Pike liked the Grimlet twins because they asked a lot of questions about cavities. Specifically, they wanted Dr. Pike to tell them how they might cause cavities in other people. What would happen, say, if they managed to put sugar into sugar-free gum? Or if they managed to get the fluoride out of fluoride toothpaste?

Dr. Pike never answered because she didn't want to encourage the wicked Grimlet twins in their wicked ways. But sometimes at night she'd dream that the Grimlet twins had succeeded in their dastardly plans and that she had patients needing root canals and multiple fillings lining up around the block. When she awoke, she'd find herself smiling a big, toothy grin.

Wednesday

It was Wednesday, the most ordinary day of the week, and the only day of the week that was neither at the beginning or the end. If Jane were a day of the week instead of a ten-year-old girl, she was sure she would be a Wednesday, just as she was sure if she were a kind of fruit that she'd be one of those dull red apples that don't taste like anything, and if she were a color, she'd be beige or maybe clear.

This particular Wednesday was more ordinary than usual. Even Ms. Schnabel, Jane's fifth-grade teacher, seemed to be feeling the effects of the day's overwhelming ordinariness. She looked across the mostly empty classroom and said, "I don't know why I bother," in a despairing voice just as if Jane wasn't there. Then Ms. Schnabel walked out of the classroom and headed down the hall to the teachers' lounge to get a cup of coffee and to see about trading her defensive linebacker for Coach Dunder's up-and-coming cornerback.

Of course, Ms. Schnabel's sudden departure from the room didn't make this Wednesday any more interesting than it already wasn't. Ms. Schnabel was always asking herself why she bothered and then wandering off to the teachers' lounge for coffee and fantasy football trades on Wednesdays. And once again, Jane was left all by herself in the classroom with nothing to do but answer the questions about storm clouds on the science work sheet Ms. Schnabel had given her before she left. It was the same work sheet on storm clouds that Jane had to answer last Wednesday, because Ms. Schnabel had forgotten that she'd already given it to her.

Jane looked out the window hoping she might at least catch a glimpse of some real storm clouds, which—while not necessarily interesting—would at least be better than answering questions about them on a work sheet. But the weather was remarkably fine that day, as it often was.

In the distance, Jane could see the tall, castlelike

building that was home to Remarkable's School for the Remarkably Gifted. She imagined that her sister and brother were having a fabulous, nonboring day at their fabulous, nonboring school. They probably hadn't even bothered to notice how interesting this Wednesday wasn't.

She took a deep breath, which she was planning on using to exhale a long, bored sigh, when suddenly she saw a straw wrapper float into the classroom through the open window. The wrapper glided toward her and landed gently on top of her desk.

Jane was so surprised that it took her a moment to notice that there was tiny spiky handwriting on the straw wrapper. She squinted at it.

"GET READY," it read in all-capital letters.

"Ready for what?" Jane wondered.

BOOM!

The sound came from the direction of Remarkable's School for the Remarkably Gifted.

The sound was followed by smoke—blue smoke—which billowed out of the school's doors and windows. The school's fire alarm blared loudly, and all of the students came running outside. Jane ran to the window to get a closer look.

The blue smoke, which had settled like a great blue storm cloud around the school, slowly drifted away. But somehow, the color blue lingered. The outside of the school was now blue, and the playground and everything in it—like the jump ropes and tetherballs and swing sets and slides—had turned blue, too. The big yellow school bus that had been parked in the asphalt-colored parking lot was now a big blue school bus parked in a blue parking lot.

Jane saw the esteemed Dr. Presnelda, headmistress of the gifted school, emerge from the building. Somehow she alone had retained her normal color. She shouted for calm as she strode through the crowd of panicked gifted students, who all suddenly seemed to have blue hair and blue skin and be wearing blue clothes.

And then a second straw wrapper—a blue straw wrapper—came drifting in through the window and landed on Jane's desk.

"HA HA HA!" the tiny writing on the wrapper read. "SEE YOU SOON."

The Captain

It did not take the esteemed Dr. Presnelda long to determine that the Grimlet twins were responsible for the disruption at the gifted school. The evidence of their guilt was overwhelming. They'd been caught blue-handed with seventeen empty bottles of bluing rinse and wide wicked grins on their nefarious faces. And just in case anyone suspected that they might still be innocent, they'd prepared a signed confession, written on blue vellum paper in blue fountain-pen ink and covered in their sticky blue fingerprints. "IT WAS US!" the confession read. "BWAH-HAH-HAH-HAH! SINCERELY, MELISSA AND EDDIE GRIMLET."

The only thing left to do was to decide how to

punish them. Dr. Presnelda arranged for an emergency meeting to be held at the school that night, and then went home to prepare herself.

Dr. Presnelda lived with Ms. Schnabel in a small yellow house near the library. They happened to be sisters, although most people never guessed this since their address was the only thing they had in common. Ms. Schnabel was tall and tended to slouch. Dr. Presnelda was quite short but had perfect posture. Ms. Schnabel usually had a glum expression on her face as if she were perpetually unhappy, while Dr. Presnelda was almost always wearing a smug, self-satisfied smile. Ms. Schnabel rarely found anything to laugh about, but when she did, the whole town could hear her deep, bellowing guffaws. Dr. Presnelda had no sense of humor whatsoever and, consequently, never laughed at all.

The two sisters had never liked each other very much, and they only spoke to each other when it absolutely necessary. So Ms. Schnabel was quite surprised when Dr. Presnelda knocked on her bedroom door.

"You're going to be late if you don't start getting ready soon," Dr. Presnelda told her. "And you know mother always said it was rude to be late."

"Late for what?"

"For the emergency meeting I've called at the gifted school. I need to discuss how I plan to punish the Grimlet twins."

"Why should I care? They didn't turn my school blue," Ms. Schnabel said. She was reading a book on Sir Francis Drake and didn't want her evening disrupted.

"You should care because . . . because . . . oh never mind!" Dr. Presnelda pursed her lips as though she'd like to say something more but didn't dare. Then she walked out of the room and slammed the door behind her.

Although Dr. Presnelda never had much to say to her sister, she tended to be long-winded in most other situations. And because she enjoyed having other people listen to her almost as much as she enjoyed the sound of her own voice, she'd made the emergency meeting mandatory for all parents of gifted-school students.

Jane's parents knew the meeting was likely to last a very long time, so they asked Grandmama Julietta Augustina and Grandpa John to come over to make sure that Jane, Anderson, and Penelope Hope did their homework and got to bed at a reasonable hour. Grandmama Julietta Augustina was only too happy to spend time with her grandchildren, but she did think Dr. Presnelda was overreacting.

"Hmph!" Grandmama said to no one in particular, even though Jane was standing right in front of her. "Not much of an emergency, if you ask me." She wasn't the least bit impressed by the fact that the Grimlet twins had turned an entire school blue, or even that they'd somehow managed to specially reformulate the bluing rinse so that it wouldn't wash off. Anderson Brigby Bright Doe III and Penelope Hope Adelaide Catalina had spent hours scrubbing their skin and shampooing their hair, but they were still just as blue as before.

Grandpa John disappeared into the kitchen to cook everyone a nice dinner of plain noodles and unbuttered toast. But just as soon as he was out of sight, Jane's grandmother forgot all about him and picked up the phone to order dinner from Remarkable's House of Otherworldly Pizza.

Exactly three minutes after Grandmama placed the order, the doorbell rang. Jane went to answer it, expecting that the pizza had arrived. Remarkable's

House of Otherworldy Pizza had the fastest pizza delivery anywhere. Madame Yvette Gladiola, who owned the pizza parlor, was psychic and could see the future. She knew who would be ordering pizza from her before they knew it themselves.

But when Jane answered the door, she didn't see the Otherworldly Pizza delivery driver standing on the front porch. Instead, she saw a pirate.

At least Jane was pretty sure the man on the porch was a pirate. He was wearing a big pirate's hat, had a large green parrot on his shoulder, and had not one, but two peg legs.

"Ahoy," the pirate said politely. The parrot on his shoulder said nothing, but gave Jane a sideways stare.

"Ahoy," Jane replied. ". . . er, I mean, hello."

"Me name be Captain Archibald Rojo Herring," the pirate said. "I be seeking the architect that lives in this 'ere house. Be she available?"

"Oh," said Jane. "I'm afraid my mother's not home right now."

"Arggh!" the pirate said. "That be a shame. Will ye be expecting her back in her home port soon?"

"No, not for a while I'm afraid. Can I give her a message?"

"Arggh!" the pirate said again, and then he sat down on the front porch to rest his weary peg legs. "Perhaps you could help me then. I be looking for the new fine bell tower that she built as an addition to the post office—but, blimey, I can't seems to find it anywheres."

"Jane? Who's at the door? Is it the pizza?"

Grandmama Julietta Augustina came to see what was taking Jane so long. When she saw the pirate, her eyes narrowed. Grandmama Julietta Augustina did not approve of pirates.

"Who are you?" she demanded. Captain Rojo Herring took off his hat and bowed.

"Captain Rojo Herring, at your service, ma'am. And this be me parrot, Salzburg."

"And what, might I ask, is a pirate captain doing in Remarkable?"

"He came to see the bell tower," Jane explained.

"Well, it hasn't been built yet," Grandmama told him. "We had some complications in the planning stage."

"I be sorry to hear that," Captain Rojo Herring said. "A lovely town like this deserves to have a lovely bell tower."

"Hmph!" Grandmama Juliette Augustina said. She still didn't approve of pirates, but she always had a soft spot for people who spoke highly of Remarkable. "Seems a shame you've come all this way for nothing. Come inside and have dinner with us. Bring that bird, too."

The pirate took a moment to consider her offer, and the parrot on his shoulder snapped its beak at the tip of his ear. Jane didn't know much about parrots, but she thought this one looked hungry.

"Thank ye," the pirate said, nervously covering his ear with his hand. "We don't mind if we do."

A Pizza and a Pirate

There was plenty of food for dinner that night. Just as Grandpa John finished cooking a big pot of noodles and a stack of plain white toast, Madame Gladiola's delivery driver showed up with an extra-large super-duper supreme pizza with all the toppings. The pizza was a whole size larger than what Grandmama had ordered, because Madame Gladiola had foreseen that the Doe family would have an unexpected dinner guest. Madame Gladiola had even sent over a small plastic container of pineapple for the parrot, and as soon as Grandmama opened it up, the parrot flew to her shoulder and began eating from it.

"Hmph!" said Grandmama Julietta Augustina. She thought the parrot was being rather impudent, but Jane noticed that she didn't try to shoo the bird away.

"Does your parrot have a name?" Penelope Hope asked Captain Rojo Herring.

"I calls her Salzburg," the pirate answered. "She won't answer to it though. But then, I don't think she like me much."

From her seat on Grandmama's shoulder, Salzburg growled at Captain Rojo Herring like an angry cat.

"Now now," Grandmama said sternly. She did not approve of growling birds. Salzburg immediately stopped and went back to eating pineapple.

The pirate had lovely table manners. He always said please and thank you, he took off his giant pirate hat before he sat down, he kept his elbows off the table, and he remembered to put his napkin on his lap. He was also much too polite to mention that Anderson Brigby Bright and Penelope Hope were blue.

"Is it true you came to Remarkable just to see the bell tower?" Penelope Hope asked Captain Rojo Herring.

"Aye, it is indeed. Bell towers be a hobby of mine."

"You can't have come across too many at sea."

"True enough," said Captain Rojo Herring. "But I love to hear them chime, I do. Such a disappointment to find out that I won't be hearing the fine sounds of yours today."

"It will be chiming soon enough," Grandmama told him.

"Ye mentioned thar be complications with its construction?"

"I'm afraid not everyone agreed that it should be built," Grandpa John told him.

"Well, blow me down," the pirate said. "Why on earth not?"

"Oh, Charles Duke Anno, the celebrated astronomer, thought we should add a planetarium to the post office instead of a bell tower," Grandmama explained. "And Dr. Bayonet wanted the space to build another glass-domed butterfly house."

"And some people think the post office looks just fine without an addition," Grandpa John added. "Some people like the post office just the way it is."

Grandmama glanced at Grandpa John with irritation. "Who thinks that?"

"Well, I do I guess," Grandpa John answered, but

by that point Grandmama Julietta Augustina was no longer paying attention to him.

Anderson Brigby Bright wasn't paying attention either. He was busy starting at the reflection of his handsome blue face in the back of a serving spoon.

"Do you think," he asked as he twisted the spoon to get a better angle on his debonair smile, "that maybe Lucinda Wilhelmina Hinojosa will finally notice me now that I'm bright blue?"

"Doesn't seem likely to me," Penelope Hope told him. "Since everyone else at the school has been turned bright blue, too."

Anderson Brigby Bright's beautiful smile drooped down to a pout. "Do you always have to be as logical as you are good at math?" he snapped, and then he ran upstairs and slammed his bedroom door behind him.

"What on earth was that about?" Grandmama Julietta Augustina asked. She did not approve of sudden departures from the dinner table.

"Anderson Brigby Bright's in love," Penelope Hope explained, rolling her eyes at the ridiculousness of it all. "Her name is Lucinda Wilhelmina Hinojosa."

"And apparently, she has perfect pitch," Jane added. "I don't know what that is, though."

"It be the ability to hear a note of music and know where it be on the musical scale," Captain Rojo Herring said. "If she hears a song, she would be able to say 'ah, that first note be a D-flat, and that second note be a G-sharp, and that third note be a middle C without even looking at the sheet music.'"

"Really?" Jane hoped he'd say more about perfect pitch, but he was distracted when Penelope Hope passed him a plate of toast. His eyes lit up when he saw it.

"I don't suppose you might have a wee smidgeon of jelly to go with the likes of this toast, would ye?" he asked. "I do likes a smidgeon of jelly with me toast."

Penelope Hope ran to the kitchen. A moment later she was back holding a big jar of violently purple jelly with a large label that read MUNCH JELLY FACTORY on one line and GENERIC FRUIT FLAVOR underneath.

"I'm sorry," she said. "This is all we have."

The pirate didn't seem to mind. He grabbed a spoon to serve himself some—but he served himself more than just a wee smidgeon. In fact, he put nearly half the jar onto his slice of toast. He took a bite and chewed it with great enthusiasm.

"Har!" he said, sounding as happy as a pirate can

sound. "This be the best jelly I ever did taste. I'll wager it be the best jelly in the whole wide world."

"Hmph!" said Grandmama, and when she "hmphed" this time, it was with so much emphasis that the pirate looked up from his toast to see how he had offended her.

"That jelly is *not* the best jelly in the world," Grandmama Julietta Augustina corrected him sternly. "That jelly will rot your teeth. We produce a much finer jelly here in Remarkable."

"Is that so?" Captain Rojo Herring said as he slathered another huge helping of generic jelly on his toast. "Well, I'll have to try to get me hands on some."

When dinner was over, Captain Rojo Herring politely thanked Jane's family for a delightful meal, gathered up his large pirate hat, and headed for the door. The parrot screeched and bit Captain Rojo Herring on the thumb when he went to take her off of Grandmama's shoulder. It was clear to everyone that Salzburg would have much rather stayed where she was.

"That's a fine bird," Grandmama said approvingly as Captain Rojo Herring and his parrot disappeared into the night. "But I don't think Captain Rojo

Herring is much of a pirate. It's such a shame. If Remarkable is going to have another pirate captain, it would be nice if he were a little more impressive."

"What do you mean, Grandmama?" Penelope Hope asked. "There aren't any other pirate captains in Remarkable."

"Never you mind, dear," Grandmama said. And she refused to speak about pirates again for the rest of the evening.

Dangerous Deeds and
Dastardly Intentions

The next day, when Jane arrived at school, she found a big surprise waiting for her. It was an even bigger surprise than finding out that Dr. Pike knew her name, having her brother and sister turn blue, or seeing a pirate on the doorstep of her house.

When Jane went to take her seat in Ms. Schnabel's room, she saw that the Grimlet twins had arrived before her, and that they were both busy defacing school property. Melissa Grimlet was carving her name on the top of her desk with the jagged edge of a broken ruler. Eddie Grimlet was drawing mustaches on important historical figures in his social studies textbook with a permanent marker.

"What are you doing here?" Jane asked. Both Grimlets looked up and gave her identically wicked grins.

"We finally managed to realize our lifelong dream of not attending the gifted school anymore," Eddie Grimlet said.

"We were expelled," Melissa said proudly. "And no one has ever been bad enough to get expelled from there before."

Ms. Schnabel was in a foul mood that morning. Given that there were only three students in the whole school, it seemed abominably and horribly unfair to her that they had all wound up in her class. And it seemed even more abominably and horribly unfair that two of the three students were the Grimlet twins. She was sure that this was her sister's way of punishing her for skipping the emergency meeting.

"I don't want any trouble out of you two," Ms. Schnabel told the Grimlet twins sternly as she sat down at her desk.

"We will be on our best behavior," Eddie said.

"You promise?" Ms. Schnabel asked suspiciously.

"Of course we do!" Melissa said. "We wouldn't want to make a bad first impression."

But what the Grimlet twins promised to do and what they actually did were two wildly different things. As soon as Ms. Schnabel's back was turned, they started making rude squeaking noises and passing notes. When Ms. Schnabel tried to confiscate the notes, Melissa Grimlet ate them.

After that, the Grimlet twins had a spitball fight, which was followed by a hair-pulling contest, which was followed by a shoving match, which resulted in a temporary truce in which they traded blue gum balls and then chewed them loudly with their mouths open.

Gum chewing, especially loud, openmouthed gum chewing, was not allowed at the public school, and so Ms. Schnabel decided to punish the Grimlet twins with a pop quiz. But they were only too happy with this punishment, since it gave them the opportunity to cheat off of each other, trading answers back and forth, and forth and back, and back and forth again until nothing they wrote on their test made any sense at all.

After the pop quiz, Melissa Grimlet complained that her stomach hurt from having eaten so much paper, and Eddie Grimlet ran with scissors.

"ENOUGH!" Ms. Schnabel bellowed. She sat down at her desk at the front of the room and sank her head into her hands. She stayed that way until the bell for recess rang.

"Yay!" shouted the Grimlet twins as they hurled themselves out of their chairs and ran off in the direction of the playground. Jane followed after them more slowly. She took the big red playground ball with her, thinking that recess might be a lot more fun now that she had someone to kick it to. The Grimlet twins, however, weren't interested in playing kickball. They had other plans.

"We have to update our Book of Dangerous Deeds and Dastardly Intentions," Melissa Grimlet explained as she took off her shoe and shook a stubby black pen out of it.

"Your what?"

"Our Book of Dangerous Deeds and Dastardly Intentions," said Eddie Grimlet, pulling a big black notebook with big black pages out of his backpack. "It's a book where we record every crime we've ever committed so we don't lose track. It's also where we write down our plans and schemes for future ill deeds so we don't forget what we're plotting."

"Oh," Jane said again. "I see."

But she didn't see, not really. When the Grimlet twins opened the book, it didn't seem to her as if anything had ever been written on any of the pages. They were all as blank and black as if the big notebook were still new.

"Now what did we do today?" Melissa mumbled to herself as she scrawled her handwriting across the pages of notebook. "Chewed gum in class, ate paper, ran with scissors, cheated on a test . . ."

"Don't forget the spitball fight," Eddie said helpfully.

Melissa Grimlet dutifully made a note of the spitball fight.

"Is your pen working?" Jane asked, noticing that as Melissa Grimlet wrote, the pen didn't seem to be leaving any words on the blank black pages.

"Oh, yes," Melissa said. "I'm just writing with invisible ink. That way no one can read what we're planning."

"Not even us," Eddie said.

The Grimlet twins plotted and scribbled in their book until recess was over. As the bell rang, Jane jumped up to go inside, but promptly fell on her face when she took her first step. Somehow, either Eddie or Melissa had managed to tie her shoelaces together when she wasn't looking.

After recess the twins did something truly diabolical—they behaved themselves for the rest of the day. It might seem like this would have made Ms. Schnabel ecstatic, but it did not. It only made her think that they were busy planning something truly dreadful. And the quieter and better behaved they were, the more she was sure that something awful was about to happen. Poor Ms. Schnabel had to leave the classroom several times to steady her nerves by blowing into a brown lunch sack, and when the bell rang at the end of the school day, it startled Ms. Schnabel so much that she leaped out of her seat as if another blue bomb had gone off.

The Grimlet twins were still so busy chortling about it as they walked home that they could barely be bothered to shove each other off the sidewalk.

"What should we do tomorrow?" asked Melissa. Her squinty eyes were gleaming.

"I think we should stage a paste-eating contest," Eddie said. "Then one of us could pretend to have paste poisoning. Jane, you could help if you want."

"Oh, I don't know about that," Jane said nervously. "I don't want to get in trouble."

"Sometimes it's nice getting into trouble."

"But, what if it upsets Ms. Schnabel?" Jane asked. "I don't want her to think I don't like her." The Grimlet twins shook their heads at Jane and sighed identically wicked sighs.

"It is strange how the victims of our criminal impulses always seem to think we don't like them," said Eddie Grimlet.

"Quite often, the victims of our criminal impulses are the very people we like the most," Melissa Grimlet added, patting Jane on the back.

By this time, they were in front of the Grimlets' creepy black house. Jane was once again hoping that maybe today they would invite her inside, but they didn't. They ran down the weedy sidewalk and disappeared behind the front door without even bothering to say good-bye.

Jane felt different that day as she walked the rest of the way home. She might be just as ordinary as ever, but for once something interesting had happened to her. It even seemed to Jane that people in town were noticing her just a little bit more than they ever had before. She was almost certain that Mr. Filbert had very nearly called after her as she passed his grocery store.

When she got to the front porch of her house, however, she figured out that people hadn't been staring at her at all. They were staring at a piece of paper that Melissa Grimlet had taped to her back.

It was a sign, and it read "JANE IS A TEACHER'S PET!" in great big letters. Underneath, in very small letters so faint that they might almost have been written in invisible ink, were the words "BUT WE HOPE WE CAN BE FRIENDS ANYWAY."

Tea with the Pirate Captain

Jane could hardly wait until dinnertime. Tonight, when her mother asked her how school was, she could share the news that the Grimlet twins were now in her class. But her gleeful anticipation of how surprised everyone would be was suddenly interrupted by a loud noise.

CRASH!

And this crashing noise was followed by the sound of a slamming door, then flapping wings, then three loud squawks, and finally Grandmama's angry voice.

"Confound you, bird! Get away from me!"

Grandmama had just come through the front door, and Captain Rojo Herring's parrot had come in

64

with her. She was fluttering around the entryway of the house, trying to land on Grandmama's shoulder, and Grandmama was wildly shooing her away with a folded newspaper. Salzburg dodged her swings, and Grandmama knocked over an umbrella stand.

"Now see what you've done, parrot!"

"Is everything okay, Grandmama?" Anderson Brigby Bright Doe III asked. He'd been painting in the backyard, but came inside to see what all the commotion was. Penelope Hope Adelaide Catalina peeked out from the kitchen, and Jane's father came out of his office.

"This ridiculous bird has been following me all day," Grandmama said, glaring as the parrot settled onto her shoulder. "I can't seem to get rid of her."

"Does Captain Rojo Herring know?" Penelope Hope asked.

"Of course he knows," Grandmama said impatiently. "I've called him three times today and asked him to order his bird to leave me alone. But he said there wasn't any point since the parrot never listens to him. Have you ever heard of such a thing? A pirate who can't control his own bird? How did he control his own ship?"

No one had an answer for her, even though Jane wondered if maybe controlling a parrot and controlling a pirate ship required very different skills.

"I have to attend to another ridiculous letter about Lucky from the Scottish Parliament," Grandmama continued, "and this feathered menace is distracting me beyond reason."

"Do you want me to take her home for you, Mom?" Jane's dad volunteered. "I could take a little break as a reward for all of the brilliant writing I've been doing on my novel today."

"Er . . . no. That's all right," Grandmama said. She knew her son well enough to realize that he was more likely to lose Salzburg in the woods or absentmindedly stuff the poor bird in a mailbox than actually deliver her safely to Captain Rojo Herring. "It seems a shame to interrupt you when you're working, especially if it's going well."

"True," he agreed. Then he looked over at his children. "One of you can do it, can't you?"

"I wish I could help," Anderson Brigby Bright said, "but I'm working on my most brilliant masterpiece ever. I can't risk losing my inspiration."

"And I'm estimating the final construction costs of

the bell tower for Mom," Penelope Hope said. "She has it marked on her to-do list for today, and you know how she gets when something on her to-do list doesn't get finished."

Everyone turned to look at Jane, who couldn't help noticing how the only time her family ever seemed to care that she was around was when they wanted her to do something that no one else wanted to.

"I don't even know where Captain Rojo Herring lives," Jane protested.

"He just moved into the Mansion at the Top of Remarkable Hill. Apparently, he's decided to stay in town for awhile," Grandmama Julietta Augustina said as she shooed Salzburg onto Jane's shoulder. "Now, go on. It'll do you good to make yourself useful."

Jane opened her mouth to complain, but then closed it again. It would only lead to an argument, and Grandmama was as good at winning arguments as she was at everything else.

The Mansion at the Top of Remarkable Hill had stood empty for as long as Jane could remember. She'd heard that was haunted by a thousand ghosts, cursed by a beautiful gypsy woman, and dripping with an evil black mold. It was also rumored to have a creaky staircase, very drafty hallways, and a cracked foundation. Normally, she would have been excited to get a chance to see inside, but at that moment, Jane was too busy feeling sorry for herself to feel much else.

"Why should I get stuck with extra chores just because I can't paint and I'm not good at math?" she grumbled as she toiled up to the top of Remarkable Hill. The path was steep and winding, and she wondered how Captain Rojo Herring ever managed it with his two peg legs. Her regular, non–peg legs were aching from the climb.

Salzburg did not answer her. The parrot was mutinously grinding her beak and muttering to herself, as she had been ever since Grandmama had sent them on their way.

As Jane reached the top of the hill, she stepped off the path for a moment to catch her breath. And in that moment, she suddenly found herself being yelled at.

"Arghh!" said a gruff voice. "Arghh! Who goes there? Who be trespassing in me vegetables?"

Jane looked down and saw that when she'd stepped off the path, she'd stepped into the mansion's garden.

Even worse, she realized she'd just trampled a bed of Greek oregano plants.

"Get yer landlubbing feet out of me heirloom herbs or I'll have you keelhauled!" the angry voice continued.

"Sorry," Jane said as she scrambled to the garden's edge.

"Young Jane? Be that you?" the voice asked, sounding suddenly much nicer, and Jane recognized it as belonging to Captain Rojo Herring.

"Yes, it's me," Jane answered. "I have your parrot. Grandmama asked me to bring her back to you."

"Arggh!" the pirate said. "She be a scurvy wee thing. Bring her aboard."

Jane expected the pirate to open the back door for her, but he did no such thing. Instead, he lowered a gangplank out of one of the windows. It wobbled a little as Jane walked up it.

If Jane had been hoping to see skulls, mold, ghosts, or general decrepitude when she stepped over the windowsill, she was soon disappointed. The room she entered wasn't just pleasant, it was also pleasantly normal. There were bookcases with books on the shelves and potted ferns on top. There was a set of lovely, overstuffed chairs on a round rug. In one corner was a baby grand piano, and in another was a telescope on a tripod that pointed out the window Jane had just come through.

Salzburg was not happy about finding herself back home with Captain Rojo Herring. When the captain took her off of Jane's shoulder, Salzburg immediately let out an angry squawk and tried to bite him on the nose. Captain Rojo Herring managed to wrestle her into a large birdcage on a stand by the piano.

"HMPH!!!!" Salzburg shouted as Captain Rojo Herring latched the birdcage door. In the struggle Salzburg had lost some feathers, which drifted down around the pirate like big green snowflakes.

"I'm sorry I was trespassing," Jane said. "And I'm sorry I trampled your herb garden."

"Now don't be getting yer stern line in a twist," the pirate said. "The likes of you be always welcome to trample me herbs. There be other types o' people I wants to keep at more than a yardarms length away, if ye take me meaning."

"What other people?" Jane asked, not taking his meaning at all.

"Why, other pirates, of course. I despise them all

now, and everything else about the pirating life besides. Now, I was just about to sit down to me tea. Could I be offering you some?"

"Um. Okay," Jane said.

He disappeared into his kitchen, and while Jane waited for him to come back, she walked over and peeked through the telescope. It was aimed at the post office. She could see Taftly Wocheywhoski, the construction foreman for the bell tower, bustling around with his survey crew.

When Captain Rojo Herring returned, he was carrying a tray with a big pot of tea, a big plate of toast, and three brand-new jars of Munch's Generic Jelly.

"How lovely," Jane said politely, but privately she was scandalized. People in Remarkable didn't buy jelly from Munch unless they had to, and they certainly wouldn't be caught dead buying three jars at once.

"It be the least I could do after you stirred yourself to bring me pesky friend back to me," Captain Rojo Herring said. "I know ye must have more important things to be doing with yer time."

"Like what?" Jane asked, genuinely puzzled.

"I hear yer brother be a fine painter, and yer sister is

master of all things numerical. So I've been assuming that ye must have some special skill you spend all of yer time at. So tell me, what is it that you be known for?"

Jane scowled down at her plate and said nothing. And even if she had said something, her answer still would have to be "nothing."

"Let me guess," the pirate continued, squinting at Jane as if this would somehow help him see her talents. "You have a flair for lion taming?"

Jane shook her head.

"Figure skating?"

"No," said Jane.

"Perhaps you knows how to do jigsaw puzzles blindfolded? Maybe you be a card shark?"

"Not me."

"Ye can climb trees better than a cat? Ye play the harmonica so that it sounds like the wind coming down a fine hill? Perhaps ye do magic tricks that baffle and amaze all who see 'em?"

"My parents argue about it sometimes," Jane said. "My mother thinks I'm a late bloomer, but my dad thinks I just haven't realized my true potential."

"Well, which one of them be right?" Captain Rojo Herring asked.

"Neither," said Jane. "I'm not good at anything, and I probably never will be."

"So you're ordinary, eh?" the pirate said. "Well, that be a fine thing to be. A mighty fine thing."

Jane looked up at the pirate to see if he was joking, but his face was quite serious.

"No, it's not," she told him. "It's actually quite boring."

"Thar be a time in me own life once when I had a chance to be ordinary, but no, I had to run off to do something special. Aye, but thar be days when I looks back and regrets it still."

"Why?" Jane asked, not quite believing him. "I'd love to be good at something. Then maybe people would finally notice me."

"But what if ye grow weary of doing what you are good at all the livelong day? What if doing something well doesn't make ye happy?"

Jane looked at the pirate, surprised. "I don't know. Do people get bored of doing things they are good at?"

"Aye," the pirate said wearily. "Aye, they can. And it be a sad thing, too. Because they've been doing what they are good at for so long that they don't know what else they might do with their lives."

"Is that what happened to you?" Jane asked. "Did you get bored with being a pirate captain?"

"Something like that," he said. "But mostly, I want to put me pirate days behind me and look for something else to fill me days. I'm going to learn all those things I never had time for—like riding a bike and learning to swim."

"You never learned to swim?" Jane asked. "Wasn't that dangerous when you were living on your pirate ship?"

The captain looked sheepish. "Aye. I just had to make sure I never fell overboard, now didn't I?"

A clock from somewhere inside the house chimed four times. "It's late," Jane said. "I think I'd better get home."

"Are ye sure? There's still a little bit o' jelly left."

"You can have it," Jane said. "Thank you very much for the tea."

"It be my pleasure," Captain Rojo Herring replied as he happily ladled the last of his jelly onto some toast.

A Bit about the Jelly

To most people, jelly is not very controversial. It is just jelly after all—something to spread on biscuits, eat on sandwiches with peanut butter, or fill the middle of jelly-filled donuts. But in Remarkable, jelly was remarkably important, and it was remarkably important because it was the source of one of Remarkable's most vexing problems.

The problem wasn't with Remarkable's locally produced jelly. Remarkable's Finest Jelly came from organic fruit grown in a picturesque orchard at the edge of town that was watered with the pure, natural spring water that bubbled up delightfully from Remarkable Springs. The fruit was picked at the peak of its freshness, and then cooked by renowned celebrity jelly chef Caspar Snikerdeski Despartie in his own kitchen using a secret recipe handed down through his family for generations.

Once the jelly had finished cooking, it was packed lovingly into handblown glass jars, and these jars were decorated with a single silver ribbon tied in a perfect bow. The jelly was a lovely color, had a marvelously smooth texture, and a taste so delicate that it almost didn't taste like jelly at all.

The jelly made in the nearby town of Munch, on the other hand, was made in a huge jelly factory out of concentrated, processed, conventionally grown fruits of dubious origin. This dubious fruit was smashed into an even more dubious goo by a large machine, and then filled with sugar, preservatives, artificial colors, and fillers. Then, another big machine glurped it into plain plastic jelly jars, and the jars were sent off to supermarkets all over the country to be sold very cheaply.

The jelly from Munch was lumpy, had a horrible fluorescent color, and smelled like artificial flavorings. But the jelly had one quality that the people from Remarkable never could explain. For all of its artificiality and its careless mass production, the jelly from Munch tasted wonderful. It tasted so good, in fact, that many people secretly wondered if it wasn't almost nearly as good as the jelly made in Remarkable.

No one would admit this out loud, of course. It was a matter of civic pride. But every now and then someone from Remarkable would pick up a jar at the store and bring it home to eat. If anyone asked about it, they made up some excuse or another—like "Oh, they were out of Remarkable's Finest Jelly at the store today. I had to get this instead," or "Oh, I must have knocked this into my shopping cart by mistake," or "Oh, I accidentally won it as a consolation prize in a candlepin bowling contest." But of course, whoever bought the jar of jelly would gobble up every last bite just as soon as no one was watching.

The fact that the people of Remarkable couldn't admit to liking jelly from Munch as a point of civic pride wasn't good for Munch's civic pride at all. The people who lived in Munch worked very hard in their jelly factory, and it bothered them that everyone from Remarkable acted like their jelly wasn't good enough to eat, even though they secretly ate gallons of it.

To make matters worse, the town of Remarkable

had managed to acquire something that the town of Munch wanted very badly—and that was a good dentist. Many of the townspeople there had terrible teeth, which wasn't surprising, given that the fumes from the jelly factory were so sweet that breathing the air in Munch was like inhaling sugar.

The people of Munch had been planning to offer Dr. Pike a position as the town's dentist, but Mayor Doe had gotten to her first. It was frustrating, but Mayor Kate Chu, the mayor of Munch, was a fair-minded person and recognized that it was her own fault for not asking Dr. Pike sooner. Still, she didn't see why Remarkable needed the best dentist in the country when it barely needed a dentist at all.

Unfortunately, no one had ever bothered to explain the long and bitter jelly rivalry to Captain Rojo Herring. And because the pirate didn't know about it, he had no idea how much trouble he was about to cause when he dialed the toll-free number for the Munch Jelly Factory and asked if he could have an entire truckload of jelly delivered to his house.

Captain Rojo Herring made the phone call right after Jane left. His teeth had begun to ache, which made him think about jelly, and this reminded him that he had finished up all of the jelly from Munch at tea. He like the jelly from Munch so much that he'd never bothered to try Remarkable's Finest Jelly, and he ate so much of the jelly from Munch that he was always having to run to Filbert's Fine Grocery Store to pick up a few more jars. Going to the store that often was hard on his peg legs, and besides, he was tired of the disapproving looks the grocery store clerk gave him when he went through the checkout line.

Right after Captain Rojo Herring placed his order, Mayor Kate Chu got a call from one of the plant managers at the jelly factory.

"Just thought you should know that a citizen from Remarkable has ordered an entire truckload of jelly for his own personal consumption," the jelly plant manager told the mayor.

"Is that right?" Mayor Kate Chu said, and then she immediately called Mayor Julietta Augustina Doe to ask if her position on Munch's jelly had changed.

"Of course not, why should it have?" Grandmama Julietta Augustina snapped. She sounded crosser than she needed to, because she was drinking out of a leaky coffee mug that Jane had made for her in pottery class, and it had dribbled hazelnut cappuccino onto the official correspondence she'd received from the Scottish Parliament. The letter was full of words like *Cease and Desist* and *False claims made about superiority of alleged lake monster* and mentioned the possibility of an ugly international incident.

"I'll have to call you back." She hung up abruptly on Mayor Chu and shouted for Stilton, her highly proficient secretary, to bring her some paper towels. The Scottish Parliament was always sending her letters like this, and she always found them annoying.

Mayor Chu didn't know about the leaky coffee mug or the letter from the Scottish Parliament, so she thought that Mayor Doe was just being rude. And if Mayor Doe wasn't going to be civil, then Mayor Chu decided she didn't need to be civil either. She shouted for her secretary to bring her a pen and paper so that she could write a letter of her own.

Mayor Chu's letter went out in the mail that afternoon. By the next morning, it had arrived at Remarkable's undistinguished post office. There, it was promptly sorted and handed off to a remarkably efficient mail carrier, and just before lunchtime, the letter was delivered to Dr. Josephine Christobel Pike, DDS.

Asta Magnifica's Day at School

For the next several weeks, Mayor Kate Chu sat in her office and stared at the phone, hoping against hope that Dr. Pike would call in reply to her letter. In her more optimistic moments, she gleefully allowed herself to anticipate Mayor Doe's reaction when she discovered the lengths that she, the mayor of Munch, was willing to go to in order to defend the honor of her town's jelly. She'd make Mayor Doe admit what everyone in Munch already knew—that their jelly was better than any jelly ever produced in Remarkable.

Meanwhile, Grandmama Julietta Augustina had no reason at all to suspect that Mayor Chu was plotting against her. Everything in her fair town was running as smoothly as ever. The citizens were happy and thriving, construction on the bell-tower addition was ahead of schedule and below budget, and most importantly, Remarkable's School for the Remarkably Gifted was nearly back to being as excellent as ever. Every inch of the building, playground, and parking lot had been scrubbed thoroughly, and the school was mostly school-colored again instead of blue.

The students were almost back to being student-colored as well. Jane had watched as Anderson Brigby Bright Doe III and Penelope Hope Adelaide Catalina's hair and skin gradually faded from dark blue to light blue, and then to lilac, then lavender, then to pale cerulean, until they were finally back to looking like their remarkable selves again. It was a good thing, too, since the Science Fair Dance was only a few weeks away, and they wanted to look their best for it.

Jane wished she were going to the Science Fair Dance, but she didn't mind being in the public school nearly as much as she had before. School was exciting now. The Grimlet twins were up to something nearly every minute, and when they weren't up to some-thing, they were plotting something, and when they weren't plotting something, they were writing down their latest crime in The Book of Dangerous Deeds and Dastardly Intentions. One day, the Grimlet twins turned all the desks upside down and glued them to the floor when Ms. Schnabel's back was turned. Another day they disorganized the periodic table, de-alphabetized the dictionary, and renumbered the rulers, all before lunchtime.

Then there was the time that Ms. Schnabel left the room for just a quick minute to check her fantasy football standings. In that minute, the Grimlet twins managed to build a small volcano out of modeling clay, poured sixteen different colors of paint down into its cone, and then filled it full of baking soda, vinegar, and a secret ingredient Melissa claimed would give it more *oomph*. The volcano erupted just as Ms. Schnabel came back. Big globs of multicolored paint splattered in all directions.

"Hooray!" the Grimlet twins shouted as they skipped around the room. "Huzzah! It worked!"

Jane thought the room looked rather pretty with bright paint splatters all over it, but Ms. Schnabel was not pleased at all. She thought about sending the Grimlet twins to the principal. She thought about making them stand in the corner. She thought about making them write "I will not build volcanoes out of clay and load them with paint, vinegar, baking soda, and a secret ingredient to give it more *oomph* when Ms. Schnabel steps out of the room for a quick minute." four thousand times each on the blackboard. But she knew none of these punishments would work. The Grimlet twins were impervious to punishment.

"Incorrigible! You two are incorrigible!" she finally shouted at them.

Melissa Grimlet stopped skipping in midstride.

"You really think so?" she asked.

"You are the most incorrigible students I've ever met!" Ms. Schnabel yelled.

The Grimlet twins were so pleased by this that they behaved themselves two whole days just to show Ms. Schnabel their appreciation. But by Thursday, they were back to their old tricks.

"A dog ate my homework," Eddie Grimlet said when he came into the classroom.

"Mine too," Melissa said.

"A dog, huh?" Ms. Schnabel said. "You expect me to believe that?"

They did expect Ms. Schnabel to believe it, but they had guessed she wouldn't, so they had taken the precaution of bringing the dog to school and feeding her Jane's homework while Ms. Schnabel watched.

"Hey!" Jane said indignantly. As much as she liked dogs, she didn't want her homework gobbled up by one—not even by this particular dog, which was a prizewinning basset hound named Asta Magnifica.

Ms. Schnabel longed to go to the teachers' lounge and soothe her nerves with a nice cup of coffee, but she didn't dare leave the Grimlets alone in the classroom again. She spent the rest of the day glaring at them; the twins spent the rest of the day looking innocent, and Asta Magnifica spent the rest of the day at the back of the classroom eating blackboard erasers.

When the school bell rang at the end of the day, the Grimlets raced outside to the playground. As soon as they were gone, Ms. Schnabel let her head sink down onto the top of her desk. She wished it were Friday. Then she wouldn't have to face being a teacher again for two whole days.

"Um . . . Ms. Schnabel?"

She lifted her head and saw that Jane was still there. With the commotion that the Grimlet twins had been causing all week, she'd completely forgotten about Jane.

"Yes?"

"Um . . . do you want me to take Asta Magnifica home? I bet Mrs. Belphonia-Champlain is worried about her."

"Who?"

"Mrs. Belphonia-Champlain. She's Asta Magnifica's owner."

Ms. Schnabel looked across the classroom and saw that Asta Magnifica was now eating a wall map of South America. She'd already chewed through most of Chile and Argentina and was just starting on Uruguay.

"I don't mind," Jane continued. "I really like dogs, you see. I asked for one for my birthday, but my parents forgot about it."

"Your parents forgot your birthday?"

"No, not this year," Jane said. "They just forgot I wanted a dog. Anyway, I'd really enjoy walking Asta Magnifica back to Mrs. Belphonia-Champlain."

Ms. Schnabel didn't say anything for a moment. She just stared out the window with that faraway look in her eyes she sometimes got. And just when Jane started to think Ms. Schnabel wasn't going to answer, she said, "I'd appreciate it, Jane. Thank you."

* * * * *

As Jane led Asta Magnifica out to the playground, she saw Melissa and Eddie huddled under the swing set, making a list in The Book of Dangerous Deeds and Dastardly Intentions.

"Copper tubing," said Eddie.

"How much, do you think?" Melissa asked.

"Oh, at least five feet."

"Did you write down the canister of carbon dioxide?" Eddie scanned the list.

"I'm not sure," he said. "It's one of the disadvantages of using invisible ink."

"How about dry ice?"

They didn't notice Jane until she'd cleared her throat several times. And once they did notice her, they slammed the book shut and tried to act like they hadn't been up to anything.

"What are you doing?" Jane asked.

"Oh, nothing," they said in unison, each trying to sound more innocent than the other.

"Really?"

The twins looked at each other and shrugged.

"It would be okay to tell her, wouldn't it?" Melissa asked.

"She is our most trusted comrade," Eddie answered.

"We're working on our weather machine," Melissa told her. "We're trying to finish it in time for the science fair."

Jane was surprised. "You're going to enter a project in the science fair? That's fantastic. Ms. Schnabel will be so pleased."

Eddie and Melissa gave her identical, disparaging looks.

"We're not going to enter our weather machine in the science fair," Eddie said. "What a revolting idea. What we're going to do is—"

Melissa kicked him hard in the shins to keep him from saying more.

"Are you busy this afternoon?" Melissa asked Jane, changing the subject. "We have grand plans. Did you know that a villainous pirate has recently moved to town?"

"Oh," Jane said. "You mean Captain Rojo Herring?"

"You know him?" Eddie asked.

"Sure. He lives in the Mansion at the Top of Remarkable Hill. Only he's not very villainous. He's really very nice."

"Don't be naive," Melissa said. "All pirates are villainous. That's why we're so excited to go meet him. Do you want to come with us?"

"I can't," Jane answered. "I'd told Ms. Schnabel that I'd take Asta Magnifica home. You could come with me, since it's your fault she's here in the first place."

"Sorry," Eddie said. "But that would involve returning to the scene of our crime, and no self-respecting criminal mastermind ever does that."

Jane told them good-bye and started walking Asta Magnifica back to Mrs. Belphonia-Champlain's house. There was nothing like taking a dog for a walk to make a person feel important. Maybe when she got home, she would remind her parents that she still wanted a dog of her own.

When she'd asked before, they hadn't told her no. Her mom had simply looked through her planner and said, "Well, Jane, I don't believe we've scheduled getting a dog this year. I can check the schedule for next year if you'd like."

"Maybe we could add it to this year's schedule," Jane pleaded. "That wouldn't be too hard, would it?"

"But aren't dogs . . . I don't know . . . a little messy?" her mom asked worriedly. Messiness would make it harder to stay organized, and it was already hard enough since she was married to a man who lost or forgot everything.

"Maybe at first, when they're still puppies. But they outgrow it. At least I think they do."

"And any dog who came to live here would need a doghouse—right? And not just any doghouse, but a really spectacular and well-designed doghouse . . ." Jane's mother's voice trailed off as she started making preliminary doghouse sketches, and Jane's heart soared with hope.

But several months later, Jane still hadn't gotten her dog. Her mother, however, had been featured in several prestigious architectural magazines for her pioneering doghouse design and had won a trophy for developing the most innovative pet product of the decade.

When Jane had asked her dad, all he had said was "You know who really needs a dog? One of the characters in my new literary masterpiece."

"But can I get a real dog, Dad? I promise I'll take care of it. I was thinking we could name it Shep or Tip, or maybe Rover . . ."

"Hmmm." He was lost in deep thought. "But I wonder what the dog in my novel should symbolize . . ." Then he'd gone back into his office and closed the door behind him without answering her question.

Trouble Comes to Town

When Mrs. Belphonia-Champlain discovered that Asta Magnifica was missing, she immediately hired Detective Burton Sly to find her. He was the greatest detective of all time, and naturally, he lived in Remarkable.

Mrs. Belphonia-Champlain suspected that Asta Magnifica had been dognapped by one of her many rivals from the dog-show circuit. She could easily imagine that Mrs. Drimm of the nearby town of Ditch might want Asta Magnifica out of the way so that her drippy-looking teacup poodle Chamomile would have a chance at winning "Best in Show" in the upcoming regional championships. Or maybe it was Mr. Tully of the town of Shrub, whose own basset hound Dribbles almost always came in second in the "Best of Breed" competition behind Asta Magnifica. And then there was Mrs. Jeeter, who lived in Squint and had a fleet of Afghan hounds that she unjustifiably thought should win more prizes than they did.

Mrs. Belphonia-Champlain did not hear the doorbell when Jane arrived with Asta Magnifica. This was because she was completely engrossed in choosing the perfect photograph of Asta Magnifica for a "Lost Pet" poster she was making. But the noise did not escape Detective Burton Sly, who'd been monitoring the phone in case the dognappers called to demand a ransom.

"Ma'am," he said. "I heard your doorbell. I believe you will find that someone has rung it."

Mrs. Belphonia-Champlain, suitably impressed with the detective's powers of deduction, went to answer the door. She was so overwhelmed with joy when she saw Asta Magnifica on her doorstep that she didn't even notice Jane.

"Oh, my poor little poopsie!" she shrieked. "How did you escape those bad dognappers? Oh, you clever pup!"

"Ma'am," said Detective Burton Sly, "if you look up, you will find that there is a small girl attached to your dog by a makeshift leash. I believe she may be responsible for your dog's safe return."

Mrs. Belphonia-Champlain, suitably impressed with the detective's power of observation, looked up and saw Jane for the first time.

"My dear child," she said, "I don't believe we've met. But I will be forever grateful to you for rescuing my poor, dear Asta Magnifica from those wicked dognappers."

Jane tried to explain that they had met many times before, and that she hadn't done anything nearly as interesting as rescuing Asta Magnifica from dognappers, but Mrs. Belphonia-Champlain was too excited to listen. She insisted on giving Jane a large reward for bringing her dog home, and had just gone off to the kitchen to get her checkbook when the phone rang.

It was Mrs. Jeeter, and she was not very happy. That afternoon, she'd discovered a strange man digging through her trash. She'd immediately set her fleet of Afghan hounds on him, and they'd chased him up a tree in a frenzy of barking, yelping, and slobbering. She'd refused to call off her dogs until the man explained that he was one of Detective Burton Sly's junior detectives and that Mrs. Belphonia-Champlain suspected that Mrs. Jeeter might be involved in the disappearance of her dog.

"Why you think I'd want to dognap your stumpy basset hound is completely beyond me!" Mrs. Jeeter shouted at Mrs. Belphonia-Champlain.

"My basset hound is not the least bit stumpy!" Mrs. Belphonia-Champlain shouted back. "You'd know that if your Afghan hounds weren't flea-bitten, bowlegged mongrels."

The two women were soon engaged in a fierce exchange of insults about the conformation, breeding, and dispositions of champion show dogs. Jane could tell that the conversation was not going to end any time soon, and she doubted that Mrs. Belphonia-Champlain would remember that she was planning to give her a reward by the time it was over. Jane nodded good-bye to Detective Burton Sly and slipped outside.

It was a shame that Jane did not get a reward for bringing Asta Magnifica back to Mrs. Belphonia-Champlain. If she had, she might have used the money to give herself a treat instead of heading straight home.

She might even have tried to get a scoop of ice cream from Mrs. Peabody's Colossal Ice Cream Palace. And if Jane had stopped there that day, she would have discovered three more pirates.

These pirates had arrived in Lake Remarkable that morning on a valiant little yawl called *The Mozart Kugeln*, which they'd sailed up from the ocean via various distributary channels. They were named Jeb, Ebb, and Flotsam—and Mrs. Peabody wasn't at all pleased to have them in her restaurant. Unlike Captain Rojo Herring, these new pirates were not meticulously dressed, and their table manners were terrible. They cursed at the prices on the menu, ate their banana splits with rusty fishing knives, and made rude faces at the other customers. When they were done eating, Flotsam beat his fist on the table to get Mrs. Peabody's attention.

"Har!" he growled. Flotsam was the shortest and meanest of the three. "I'll be wanting a word with you."

"Argghh!" the other pirates growled in agreement, and they beat their fists on the table, too.

"Well, what is it?" Mrs. Peabody asked, wrinkling up her nose as she walked over to them. The three pirates smelled very strongly of pickled squid and mildew.

"We be looking for a pirate friends of ours. He has two peg legs and a big green parrot. Have you seen the likes of him around here?"

"I'm sure I don't know who you're talking about," Mrs. Peabody said huffily. This wasn't strictly true, of course. Mrs. Peabody had seen Captain Rojo Herring that very morning. He came to her ice cream parlor almost every day, so he could sit by the window and watch Taftly Wocheywhoski and his crew work on the post office addition. She'd never seen anyone so fascinated by a construction project before. But Mrs. Peabody wasn't about to mention that Captain Rojo Herring was a regular customer, because she didn't want Ebb, Jeb, and Flotsam to think she ran the kind of ice cream parlor that was frequented by pirates.

Ebb scowled like he suspected she was lying. He was the tallest of the three and had a patch over one eye.

"Well, if you should see such a man, don't be telling him that we be asking about him," Ebb said. "He's caused us a bit o' trouble, you see. And if he finds out we're after him, he'll run again befores we can return the favor."

"And we'll be causing quite a bit of trouble ourselves if we don'ts find 'im," Jeb added between bites of ice cream. He was almost handsome, almost smart (which is a polite way of saying he was actually quite dumb) and always hungry.

Mrs. Peabody pursed her lips and put the bill for the three banana splits on the pirates' table. "You can pay at the cash register whenever you're ready," she said pointedly, hoping that they would take the hint and go.

Flotsam slapped a grubby-looking gold doubloon on top of the bill, and the three pirates walked out, laughing their mean pirate laughs.

Hmmm

"So, Jane, you aren't busy, are you?" Anderson Brigby Bright Doe III asked as Jane came down the stairs on Saturday morning. He was giving her one of his most dazzling smiles. Jane looked back at him suspiciously without answering. If she answered, she'd have to say she wasn't doing anything, and then he'd probably ask her for a favor.

"Because if you aren't busy," Anderson Brigby Bright continued, "I thought you might like to come look at my new masterpiece. I haven't showed it to anyone else yet."

"Really?" Jane asked, feeling suddenly flattered. Anderson Brigby Bright didn't normally care if she ever saw his paintings or not.

Anderson Brigby Bright's masterpiece was on an easel in the backyard and covered by a velvet sheet. As Jane stepped in front of it, he whipped the cover off with a flourish.

"Ta-da!" he shouted happily, and then he stepped back and waited for Jane's praise.

The masterpiece was a photorealistic portrait of Lucinda Wilhelmina Hinojosa. But Jane didn't think it was the best photorealistic portrait that Anderson Brigby Bright had ever painted. In real life, Lucinda Wilhelmina Hinojosa's hair was black and shiny, but in Anderson Brigby Bright's picture, her hair was ten times blacker and a hundred times shinier. Her well-shaped nose was much shapelier, and her chic little glasses were even smaller and even more chic. But the most unrealistic aspect of the portrait was Lucinda Wilhelmina Hinojosa's lips, which were stretched into a beauteous smile instead of being pressed together in a hum.

"Oh," Jane said, "it's, um, nice. Have you asked her to the Science Fair Dance yet?"

"No. Not yet. I have a plan though. I'm going to give Lucinda Wilhelmina Hinojosa this picture, and then she'll be so impressed with it that she'll ask me to the dance," Anderson Brigby Bright said confidently.

Jane, who was now used to the precise and complex schemes of the Grimlet twins, could see that this wasn't much of a plan. But there was no point in arguing with Anderson Brigby Bright about it. He'd never listen to her anyway.

"Oh," she said instead. "Well, good luck with that."

"It's going to take more than luck, Jane. I'm going to need your help, too."

"You are? Why?"

"I need someone to carry the painting over to her house for me."

Jane groaned and wished she'd locked herself in her bedroom the moment her brother had looked in her direction.

Because Anderson Brigby Bright Doe III had expansive feelings for Lucinda Wilhelmina Hinojosa, he'd painted her portrait on a very large canvas. The canvas was almost larger than Jane and was extremely difficult for her to carry—especially since Anderson Brigby Bright refused to help.

"I'm much too anxious," he told Jane. "And it would be such a shame if my masterpiece got dropped."

"Wouldn't it be easier to just ask her to the dance?" she asked, grunting under the painting's weight. Anderson Brigby Bright paled at the very idea.

"Of course not! What if she said no? I would be crushed! It's much safer to get her to ask me. I'm sure I'll say yes."

It wasn't far to Lucinda's house, but the closer Jane and Anderson Brigby Bright got, the slower they both walked—Jane, because the painting seemed to get heavier and heavier with every step, and Anderson Brigby Bright, because he was getting more apprehensive. He stood on Lucinda's porch for nearly three minutes before he had the courage to ring the doorbell, and once he pressed it, he completely lost his nerve.

"I don't think I can do it!" he squeaked dramatically.

"What do you mean?" Jane asked. But Anderson Brigby Bright wasn't there to answer her. He'd already run back down the front walk and hidden himself behind a large hydrangea bush next to the mailbox.

Jane turned to run after him, but it was too late. Lucinda Wilhelmina Hinojosa had already opened the front door. She was humming one of Johann

Hummel's trumpet concertos and didn't stop when she saw Jane on the doorstep.

"Hi," Jane said awkwardly. "I . . . uh . . . I . . ."

"Mmm-hmmm?" hummed Lucinda. "Are you here to join the search for Ysquibel?"

Jane was so surprised by the question she almost didn't know how to respond. "No . . . I, uh . . ."

"I always have my eye out for new members. I am the regional copresident of the Save Ysquibel Now! Club—or S.Y.N!C., as it is sometimes called."

"Oh. I didn't know that. What are you saving him from, exactly?"

"From being lost, of course. He is the greatest living musician in the world today. But please don't tell Ludwig von Savage I said that. He is our vice president and is sometimes rather touchy about being only the second greatest living musician."

"Hmmm," answered Jane, as if she were pondering what Lucinda Wilhelmina Hinojosa had just said. Humming was contagious. "But I'm not here about that. I'm here because my brother wanted me to give you this." She leaned the painting against a porch railing so that Lucinda Wilhelmina Hinojosa could see it.

Lucinda Wilhelmina Hinojosa looked at the masterpiece curiously, humming all the while.

"Hmmm," she said finally. "Is that supposed to be me?"

Jane was caught off guard. The painting might be overly flattering, but it was unmistakably a picture of Lucinda Wilhelmina Hinojosa.

"Don't you think it looks like you?" Jane asked.

"Hmmm. I don't know. I don't usually think about how I look. I usually just think about how I sound. Do I know your brother?"

"I think so," Jane said. "You go to school with him."

"Hmm," Lucinda Wilhelmina Hinojosa hummed in a perfect C-sharp. She always hummed in C-sharp when she was trying to remember if she knew someone. "Well, tell him thank you, I guess." And then she closed the door, leaving her enormous portrait on the porch.

Anderson Brigby Bright was beside himself with anxiety by the time Jane reached his hiding place in the hydrangea bush.

"Did she like it?" he demanded.

"Hmmm," Jane answered. "I don't know."

"Did she ask me to the dance? Did she? Did she?"

"Well, hmmm, no, not exactly," Jane said. "It never really came up."

Anderson Brigby Bright's face fell. Jane couldn't remember a time he had ever looked so disappointed. She couldn't help but think that if he'd been willing to listen to her before they left the house, then he would have known that this was exactly what she thought was going to happen. But of course, he hadn't listened to her, and now he was just terribly, terribly disappointed.

"You could draw a picture of someone else and see if they'll ask you to the dance instead," Jane suggested.

Anderson Brigby Bright shook his head stubbornly. "I want to go with Lucinda Wilhelmina Hinojosa. If I can't go with her then I don't want to go to the dance at all."

"Maybe she didn't understand what the painting was for," Jane said reasonably. "Why don't you just go ask her?"

"I've never asked anyone to a dance before. I wouldn't know how to begin." He looked up at his sister with tears in his eyes. "I don't suppose you'd ask Lucinda for me, would you, Jane? Please?"

"Why should I have to?"

"It wouldn't be nearly as hard for you to get turned down by her as it would for me. You're used to that kind of thing."

"Oh, all right," Jane said, and she walked back up the porch steps and rang the doorbell again. When Lucinda Wilhelmina Hinojosa answered this time, she was humming a Strauss waltz.

"Hmm," she said. "You're back."

"Um . . . yes," Jane said. "I was wondering . . . I was just wondering if you wanted to go to the Science Fair Dance with my brother. He'd really like to take you."

"Hmmmm," Lucinda Wilhelmina Hinojosa hummed in a perfect B-flat. She always hummed in a perfect B-flat when she was considering something. "Will there be music?"

"Oh, I expect so," Jane answered.

"Will it interfere with my search for Ysquibel?

"I doubt it."

"Hmmmm," she hummed, but this time she hummed in G, which was the note she always hummed when she'd come to a decision. "Well, okay then. Tell your brother I'd enjoy going to the dance very much."

Anderson Brigby Bright was overcome with joy when he found out that Lucinda had said yes. He ran all the way back to the mirror in his bedroom so that he could practice parting his wonderfully wavy hair for the big night.

"You're welcome," Jane called after him. But Anderson Brigby Bright didn't hear her, and Jane was left to walk home by herself.

A Bit More about the Jelly

While Jane and Anderson Brigby Bright Doe III were at Lucinda Wilhelmina Hinojosa's house, Dr. Josephine Christobel Pike was eating breakfast on her back porch.

It was a remarkably nice day for having breakfast outside. The weather was perfectly fine, and if Dr. Pike had looked up, the fabulous view of Remarkable Hill would have brought a smile to her face. But Dr. Pike did not look up. She was reading and rereading a letter she'd received a few weeks ago, and her face was scrunched up in a thoughtful frown.

The letter was an impassioned plea from Mayor Kate Chu, begging Dr. Pike to accept an offer to become the official dentist of the town of Munch. She described the tooth-related woes of the town—how so very many citizens needed root canals, dental implants, fillings, scalings, cleanings, and good stern lectures about regular flossing. Dr. Pike couldn't help but be excited by the offer. Lately, she'd even begun to wonder if her fine dentistry skills weren't getting a little rusty. But despite the lack of tooth decay in the town, Remarkable was her home now, and it would not be easy to leave.

Mayor Chu had sensed that she might need more persuading, so that morning, she'd sent a jar of Munch's Generic Jelly to Dr. Pike's house to demonstrate how sugary and cavity causing it was. Dr. Pike had brought the jar outside with her, and was planning to spread a sensibly thin layer on a piece of whole wheat toast. But she was feeling so unsettled that she picked up a spoon and ate a bite of jelly directly from the jar. The jelly was very, very sweet, and very, very good. She could understand why the people of Munch needed her services so badly.

She took another bite, and then another, and only stopped because she suddenly saw a flash of reflected sunlight coming from the direction of Remarkable

Hill. She looked up and realized that someone was watching her through a telescope.

That someone was Captain Rojo Herring. She could see him standing in the window of his mansion with the telescope pressed to his eye. Dr. Pike had never met Captain Rojo Herring, but she had seen him in town a few times hovering around the post office.

She put down her spoon, embarrassed that she'd been caught indulging in such a sugary treat, and waved to him guiltily. He waved back. Then she stood up and went straight inside to floss and brush.

Captain Rojo Herring was embarrassed that he'd been caught staring at the woman who'd been eating jelly with a spoon. He didn't know who she was, and he certainly hadn't meant to intrude on her privacy. He had only intended to check on the progress of the bell tower. The bells were supposed to be delivered soon, and he wanted to watch while they were installed.

But the area around the post office addition was quiet. The truck with the bells on it had not yet arrived. He was just about to put his telescope down when he caught a glimpse of something that was very nearly as exciting to him as the post office addition.

It was a beautiful, brand-new jar of Munch's Generic Jelly, which was sitting on top of a table on a back porch. And even more beautiful than the jar of jelly was the woman who was eating dainty spoonfuls of it. Captain Rojo Herring's heart flipflopped in his chest as he watched her spoon another bite of jelly into her mouth. Her teeth were white and perfect. He'd have bet all the pirate treasure in the world that she had the world's loveliest smile.

She looked up suddenly, as if she'd sensed him watching her. Her eyes scanned the hill above until they met his through the telescope. She put down her jelly spoon and raised a hand to wave to him. Captain Rojo Herring's face blushed red, and his peg legs went weak and wobbly. He waved back.

The woman suddenly stood up and went inside, and Captain Rojo Herring found that all he could do was stare after her. His heart had moved on from doing flipflops to cartwheels, somersaults, and happy backflips.

"Avast!" he sighed as he clutched his chest. He'd heard of love at first sight, but he'd never believed in it until just that moment.

Milk and Pizza

At six o'clock, the doorbell rang at the Doe house. When Jane answered it, she found Lucinda Wilhelmina Hinojosa on the front steps.

"Oh, hello again," Jane said. "Are you here to see my brother?"

"Hmmm," Lucinda Wilhelmina Hinojosa hummed. "I don't think so. Do I know your brother?"

"Sure. He's Anderson Brigby Bright Doe III. He's taking you to the Science Fair Dance."

"If you say so," Lucinda said. "But no. I'm not here about that. I'm here to give you this."

She was pulling a red metal wagon that was full of cartons of milk. She handed Jane one.

"Look at the back," Lucinda instructed.

Jane turned the carton around. She saw the word MISSING in large letters over a vague and out-of-focus picture of a man. And under the picture it read THE FAMOUS COMPOSER YSQUIBEL. LARGE REWARD OFFERED FOR HIS SAFE RETURN.

"You may remember," Lucinda told Jane, "that I am the regional copresident of the Save Ysquibel Now! Club. We are distributing milk cartons in our attempts to locate the great composer before the premiere of his composition for the new bell tower. There's some urgency. He's never missed one of his own premieres before."

"Oh," Jane said. "I didn't know that."

"You didn't? Hmm," she hummed disapprovingly. Lucinda couldn't believe anyone knew so little about Ysquibel. "Well, I can't stay and chat. I have more milk cartons to deliver."

Lucinda walked back down the front steps and picked up the handle of her wagon.

"Wait," Jane called. "Don't you at least want to say hi to Anderson Brigby Bright? I'm sure he'd love to talk to you."

"Who?"

"My brother. The one who is taking you to the dance."

"Does he have information on Ysquibel's whereabouts?"

"Um . . . I doubt it."

"Then what could we possibly talk about?" Lucinda asked, and she headed off down the street with her wagon in tow.

Jane carried the milk carton inside. Lucinda was the second surprise visitor to come to their house that evening. The first had been the delivery driver from Madame Gladiola's House of Otherworldly Pizza.

"There must be some mistake," Jane's father had said when he opened the door and saw the delivery driver. "We don't need pizza tonight. I'm planning on making my world-famous olallieberry pancakes."

"Madame Gladiola has foreseen your confusion," the driver said. "She said to tell you that soon you will realize that you lost your handwritten notes for your new chapter when you went to town earlier today. And your wife will realize that you accidentally picked up the bell installation instructions when you were organizing your notes on the kitchen counter, and now those are lost, too."

Jane's mother gave Jane's father a wild look.

"What! Tell me you didn't!" she shrieked. "I need those instructions! The bells arrived an hour ago!"

Jane's father gave the pizza delivery driver a wild look.

"I lost my notes? But I can't have lost them! I finally figured out how to incorporate the symbolism of the dog!"

"We have to retrace your steps," Jane's mother cried as she ran out the front door. "Your mother is going to have a fit when I tell her about this."

"You don't have to tell her, do you, dear?" Jane's father wailed as he ran out the door after her.

Her parents had been gone for a while now, which made Jane think that the hunt for the notes and the instructions wasn't going well. She couldn't help but feel a little sorry for them as she walked back into the dining room where her brother and sister were eating pizza.

"Who was at the door?" Penelope Hope asked.

"It was Lucinda Wilhelmina Hinojosa," Jane said.

"Lucinda?" Anderson Brigby Bright said. His face took on the pale, loopy look of a boy in love. "What did she want?"

"She brought us this," Jane said, setting the milk carton down in front of him.

"Is it for me? Is it a present. Did she send me some token of love?"

"Um . . . actually I think it's a . . ."

Anderson Brigby Bright grabbed the carton and looked at it.

"It's milk," he said. "Why did she bring me milk?"

"It's not about the milk," Jane tried to explain. "It's about the picture on the back."

Anderson Brigby Bright turned the carton around. "But this picture is ghastly!" he complained. "Who would choose to use an inferior photograph when they could use a photorealistic painting instead?"

"Most people," Penelope Hope told him. "At least most people who don't spend their days in front of an easel."

"Anderson Brigby Bright, are you sure you want to take her to the dance?" Jane asked. She was starting to worry that Lucinda didn't care very much about her brother, certainly not as much as she cared about being the regional copresident of S.Y.N!C. "I'm not sure that you have much in common with her."

"We are both brilliant!" Anderson Brigby Bright said indignantly. "Isn't that enough?"

Penelope Hope raised an eyebrow at him. "What are you planning to talk to her about? Her perfect pitch?"

"I assume we'll talk about the photorealistic portrait I painted of her. She must have been thrilled to get it."

"I doubt she was thrilled," Penelope Hope said. "I wouldn't want a portrait. I couldn't care less about photorealistic paintings."

"What?" Anderson Brigby Bright stammered.

"If some boy wanted to impress me, he'd have to do something important, like calculate the square root of thirteen in his head. I wouldn't ask him to a dance just because he'd drawn some silly painting."

"That's the most ridiculous thing I've ever heard!" Anderson Brigby Bright snapped.

"Square roots are never ridiculous."

"Square roots are the most ridiculous thing in the world!"

Jane looked back and forth between her brother and sister as they scowled across the table at each other. Like most geniuses, they always assumed that everyone in the world was just as interested in what they were a genius at as they were. She didn't think either one of them had ever noticed that photorealism and math were not the only things in the world that people cared about.

"Um, Anderson Brigby Bright," Jane said. "I think maybe Penelope Hope has a point. I think maybe if you want to impress Lucinda, you should do something she cares about."

Anderson Brigby Bright did not look convinced. "What would she care about more than a beautifully realistic painting of herself?"

"She seems to like music an awful lot," Jane answered.

"Oh, music," Anderson Brigby Bright said disparagingly. And even Penelope Hope agreed.

"Music is nowhere near as interesting as math."

"And math is nowhere near as interesting photorealistic paintings," Anderson Brigby Bright added.

"Math is much more interesting!"

"It's boring!"

"Portraits are boring."

"No. They're interesting!"

They spent the rest of dinner yelling at each other.

And they were still yelling when Jane went upstairs to brush her teeth and go to bed. Finally, her father came home from looking for the lost papers (which he hadn't found) and told them that their argument was boring, and that it was interrupting his plan to write new notes for his novel, which was more interesting than painting and math combined.

Shortly thereafter, Jane's mother came home (having found both the handwritten notes and the bell installation instructions in the trash at Coffeebucks) and spent some time being upset at her father for letting his boring novel interfere with the most interesting architectural project she'd ever designed.

Her father apologized, and her mother told him he'd better never lose anything of hers again or else. She had a way of saying "or else" that made it clear how serious she was. And Jane's father promised that he never would.

And then finally, all was forgiven—and the house was remarkably quiet at last.

A Crash and a Splash in the Night

Shortly after Jane fell asleep, the night air of Remarkable was filled with the sound of strange and lovely music. The music was delightfully melodic, and yet rather sad, too. Anyone lucky enough to hear it wouldn't know whether to dance a joyful jig or weep over all of life's tragedies and frustrations.

The music was coming from Captain Rojo Herring, who was leaning against a tree at the edge of Lake Remarkable and playing his beloved hardanger fiddle. A hardanger fiddle is not unlike a regular violin, but with twice as many strings. It was Captain Rojo Herring's favorite instrument for times when he needed to soothe his nerves, and nothing had ever made him as nervous as realizing he'd fallen in love with a woman whose name he did not know.

That night he played the fiddle in a way that was almost magical. The notes seemed to harmonize with the breeze moving through the forest around him. The crickets and katydids in the woods fell silent to listen to him. Even the waters of Lake Remarkable seemed to be eddying and churning to his tune.

Then the lake waters started to ripple and surge as a large shadowy creature moved beneath the water's surface. Captain Rojo Herring was so preoccupied with making music that he didn't notice. He dug deeper into his melancholy mood and played a new melody that was even more beautiful than the ones he had played before. And in response, the shadowy creature rose out of the depths, swaying gently to the sounds of the fiddle. It had a long, serpentine neck, big horns, and fierce white fangs. It stared at the captain with narrowed orange eyes.

"*ARRRGHHHH!*" screamed Captain Rojo Herring. He backed away from the edge of the lake as fast as he could.

"*AH-HOOOOO!*" screamed the creature as it

backed away from the edge of the shore and then dove back down into the lake's depths.

Captain Rojo Herring was torn between running to the water to see if the large serpentine creature he'd seen was real and running back home so he could climb into bed and hide under his covers. He clutched his fiddle so hard that all eight strings stretched under his fingers.

"I think she likes your music," came a gentle voice behind him, and Captain Rojo Herring very nearly screamed *"Arrgghhh!"* again. He hadn't noticed that Grandpa John was sitting on a rock a short distance away and holding an open packet of figgy doodles.

"Ye . . . yar . . . did ye see that monstrous thing come out of the lake?"

"Of course," Grandpa said. "That's Lucky. She often comes out on quiet nights like this one."

"But . . . but . . ." Captain Rojo Herring was having a hard time speaking because his teeth were chattering so hard. "I didn't think anyone had clapped eyes on 'er in years and years."

"Normally she hides when people are around," Grandpa said. "She doesn't seem to pay much attention to me though, but of course, hardly anyone does."

"You mean ye've seen her before, and ye've never told anyone?"

"Who would I tell?"

Captain Rojo Herring looked back out at the water. The lake monster had vanished completely. He put his fiddle to his chin and began to play it again. After a moment or two, Lucky peeked her head back out and looked at the captain cautiously.

Now that he was over his fright, Captain Rojo Herring could see that she was a beautiful creature—more than beautiful. He played the loveliest music he knew, and Lucky slowly began to swim back toward the shore.

And then, for no reason he could see, she suddenly dove back down into the lake and disappeared. He put his fiddle down and stared after her in wonder.

"Aye. That be a sight that is a privilege for any man to behold," he told Grandpa John. But Grandpa John's expression was one of worry instead of awe.

"I suppose you're going to tell everyone you've seen her now, aren't you?"

"You don't think I should?"

"No," Grandpa said. "She's very shy. It would be a disaster if you told anyone. She'd have news crews after her. The cryptozoologists will come try to capture her again, and tourists will line the edge of the lake with binoculars and video cameras. It won't end until she's been hounded to death."

Captain Rojo Herring didn't say anything. He just stared across the lake waters with a melancholy look on his face. For a moment, Grandpa feared the captain had not been listening.

"You can understand how much she'd hate that, can't you?" Grandpa asked him gently. Captain Rojo Herring turned and gave Grandpa a smile that was as sad a smile as anyone had ever smiled.

"Aye," he said quietly. "I understand too well. Her secret be safe with me."

But even as Captain Rojo Herring promised to keep Lucky safe, he himself was in considerable danger.

Jeb, Ebb, and Flotsam had been listening hard to the mysterious music and were trying to determine what direction it was coming from.

"This way, mateys," growled Flotsam as he lurched to the left, in the direction of the town. "I be certain that the music is coming from over yonder."

"*Argh!*" Ebb said, lurching right toward the jelly

orchard. "Yer ears be full of old barnacles. The music be coming from over there."

"A pox on you both," growled Jeb. "The music be coming from behind us, just likes I told you both before." And he turned around to head back up Re-markable Hill.

"Yer mad! We just came that way."

The pirates began shoving and pushing each other, each trying to get the others to go in the direction he thought was right.

"It's a'coming from that way," growled Jeb, kick-ing Ebb in the shins and shoving Flotsam's head with his elbow.

"It's not! You lily-livered sea toad," Flotsam said, grabbing Jeb's elbow and redirecting it at Ebb's nose.

"*Garrghh!*" shouted Ebb, suddenly feeling like the other two pirates were ganging up on him. He low-ered his head and charged at both of them. Jeb and Flotsam reeled backward.

Now the three pirates had been working very hard to fight quietly. But when Ebb pushed Jeb, he tripped over an azalea that was in front of a tidy yellow house and broke the flowerpot it was planted in.

Normally, this would have made a startling noise

on such a quiet night. However, in this case, the sound of the breaking pot was hardly noticeable. When Ebb pushed Flotsam, he knocked over a large recycling bin, which made the kind of horrible commotion that only occurs when crushed aluminum cans, polycarbonate containers, and glass bottles spill across a cement driveway.

In the moment of silence that followed, the three pirates held their breath, hoping that no one had heard. But then the porch light of the little yellow house came on and a lone figure stepped out into the night. It was Ms. Schnabel, wearing a pair of fluffy pink slippers and teddy bear pajamas.

"Who's there," she said in a stern, teacherly tone. The pirates cowered in the shadows of her lilac bushes.

"Whoever made this mess had better come out right now and clean it up," she said, even more sternly and more teacherly than before. It was too much for Flotsam, who screamed "run" and tore off down the street as fast as he could. Jeb and Ebb followed close behind.

Ms. Schnabel shouted and shook her fist at the three departing figures, and as she did so, she smelled the strong smell of the pirates in the night air.

Now, most people who have the misfortune of smelling the strong smell of pirates in the night air say "ew" and immediately quit breathing through their noses. But not Ms. Schnabel. She sniffed the air, and then sniffed it again, and then closed her eyes and breathed in as much of the smell as she could. The smell made her remember something—a dream she'd had when she'd been only a little older than Jane. It was a dream she'd abandoned a long time ago.

But dreams are funny things. Sometimes even the most impractical and irresponsible dreams just won't be ignored. And sometimes when you don't follow your dreams, your dreams come looking for you.

This is exactly what happened to Ms. Schnabel. She might have thought all she heard was the sound of someone making a mess of her recycling, but it was also the sound of her dream finding her after many years. And although Ms. Schnabel had no way of knowing it that night as she stood on her porch in her fuzzy pink slippers, her life was about to change.

Never Ever Trust a Pirate

The Grimlet twins were in a terrible mood on Monday. They both came stomping into the school after the tardy bell rang and miserably flung themselves into their seats. And even though Ms. Schnabel's back was to the class as she wrote the date on the chalkboard, the Grimlets couldn't rouse themselves to take advantage of it. Jane was shocked.

"I don't suppose any of you did your homework?" Ms. Schnabel asked wearily as she turned around to face another week of teaching.

"I did," Jane said. The Grimlet twins, however, just shrugged and shook their heads. They were too depressed to make any kind of smart-mouthed reply.

"Well let's hear it, you two," Ms. Schnabel said. "What's your excuse this time? Was it another dog? Some kind of explosion? Maybe you lost it during a museum heist?"

"No," Melissa said. "We didn't have enough time."

"We had to spend a big part of the weekend getting our project ready for the science fair," Eddie explained glumly.

"You expect me to believe that the two of you are doing something as law abiding as entering a science fair?" Ms. Schnabel was incredulous.

"We're not entering the science fair, we're—" Eddie started to say, but then Melissa gave him a particularly savage punch in the arm to make him stop talking.

"The rest of our weekend was wasted by the pirate captain," Melissa said.

"The pirate captain?" Ms. Schnabel said. "What pirate captain?"

"Captain Rojo Herring. We were hoping he would teach us how to become pirates. Unfortunately, when we arrived, Captain Rojo Herring was trying to learn how to ride a bicycle. He told us if we wanted to learn piracy, we had to give him bicycle lessons."

"That's wonderful," Jane said. "He's been wanting to learn to ride a bicycle."

"It wasn't wonderful," Eddie corrected her. "It was absurd. Do you know how long it takes to teach someone with two peg legs how to ride a bicycle? He must have crashed three thousand times before he made it to the end of his driveway."

"But we did it. We finally taught him how to ride," Melissa said. "And then he said that learning how to be a pirate was hard, and that it was too much work to train landlubbers like us—especially since he'd fallen in love and was going to be busy for a while."

"And that if we were interested in career development, we should go get a paper route or something. Then he rode away on his bicycle."

"That is ridiculous," Ms. Schnabel said, putting her hands on her hips. "That might just be the most ridiculous thing I've ever heard."

"Wanting to learn to be a pirate is not ridiculous," Melissa told her. "Just because you never wanted to do anything exciting doesn't mean that the rest of us are happy being locked up in a boring old classroom."

"Some of us actually enjoy doing interesting things more than we enjoy doing long division," Eddie added.

Ms. Schnabel gave the Grimlet twins a flinty stare, and it was flinty enough to startle them into sitting still, if only for a moment.

"It's ridiculous that anyone would think that you two could be entrusted with a newspaper route," Ms. Schnabel said. "And what Captain Rojo said about learning to be a pirate is just dead wrong. It's not hard at all."

"What would you know about it?" Eddie asked rudely.

"Plenty," she said. "I could teach you myself if I wanted to. And I'm quite a good teacher, too, which is something you'd know if you were actually willing to sit still long enough to learn something."

The Grimlet twins looked at each other. Melissa raised her left eyebrow, and Eddie raised his right. They conferred for a few moments, and then nodded in agreement.

"We accept," Eddie said.

"Excuse me?"

"We accept. We will start behaving in class, as long as you start teaching us about being pirates."

Ms. Schnabel glared at Eddie for a long moment. Jane held her breath, expecting her to start yelling about how she was a teacher and this was her classroom and the Grimlet twins would have to behave whether they liked it or not. But Ms. Schnabel didn't do that. She inhaled deeply and closed her eyes, almost as if she were picturing herself somewhere else.

"Har!" she said quietly, and then she opened her eyes again. It never paid to keep them closed for too long in front of the Grimlet twins.

"Do we have a deal?" Melissa demanded.

"Well that all depends," Ms. Schnabel said. "Are you willing to pledge your loyalty to me as your sworn captain? It'll have to be a blood oath."

"Well, I don't know why you should get to be captain . . ." Eddie Grimlet began, but Ms. Schnabel didn't let him finish his sentence.

"Arrrghh!" she yelled, and she pounded her fist on the desk. "Either I be the captain or we goes back to doing long division."

She sounded a lot like Captain Rojo Herring, only much, much meaner.

"Um, okay. You can be captain, I guess," Melissa said.

"All right then, me hearties. I'll start by teaching you the most important rule of pirating life."

"Rules? Pirates don't have rules, do they?" Eddie asked.

"Aye, that they do. And the most important rule be this: always do what yer captain tells you, or suffer the consequences."

And then Ms. Schnabel began to laugh—a wild, savage laugh. The sound of it made Jane very worried.

More about the Jelly and the Dentist

Grandmama Julietta Augustina walked into city hall after spending a satisfying morning at the construction site for the post office addition.

Taftly Wocheywhoski and his hardworking crew had just finished hanging all fifty-seven bells. A campanologist would arrive next Wednesday to make sure the bells were properly tuned, and on the Thursday after that, a chronometric engineer would come from the Naval Observatory in Greenwich, England, to make certain the bell tower clock kept perfect time.

"And on Friday morning, we can have the opening ceremony for the bell tower. We'll have all those extra people in town for the science fair. They'll probably

133

appreciate the chance to be part of this remarkable moment in Remarkable's history. What do you think of that, bird?"

Salzburg, who was perched on Grandmama's shoulder, bobbed her head and squawked approvingly. Grandmama Julietta Augustina had given up trying to get Captain Rojo Herring to take more responsibility for his parrot and was even starting to enjoy the bird's company.

When she arrived back at her office, Stilton, her faithful secretary, handed her a cup of coffee and three phone messages. One was from Kate Chu, who asked that Grandmama Julietta Augustina call her back about some urgent business between their two towns.

"Hmph!" Grandmama said to herself. She was certain that no business between Remarkable and Munch could ever be considered urgent. The second message was from Mrs. Peabody, who was complaining that the town was infested with pirates, and the third was from Mrs. Belphonia-Champlain, who was convinced beyond reason that the town was plagued by dognappers.

She pushed the messages aside. She needed to finish responding to the Scottish Parliament's ridiculous complaint. Although she was certain that Lucky was bigger and more elusive than Nessie—the Scottish Parliament seemed to feel she should provide some sort of proof, which was hard to obtain given Lucky's shy nature. She pulled out her most official-looking stationery and began composing her reply.

"Dear sirs and ma'ams," she wrote. "We have received your ludicrous allegations and wish, once again, to cordially inform you that we have no intention of apologizing for the fact that our lake monster is both larger and more elusive than your own. The town of Remarkable would also like to cordially suggest that if you are not comfortable with this true and indisputable fact, then you are free to go jump in a loch of your own choosing. Sincerely, Mayor Julietta Augustina Doe."

Grandmama signed the letter with a flourish. And as she was sealing it into an official envelope, she heard a discreet knock at the door.

"Madam Mayor," Stilton said. "Please excuse my interruption. But there is citizen out here who wants to talk to you."

"Who is it?"

Stilton hesitated. "I'm afraid I don't recognize him,

ma'am. But he claims that you know each other well and that you'd be upset if I didn't let him speak to you. His name is . . . oh dear. I'm afraid I've forgotten. I'll go ask him again."

"No need," Grandmama Julietta Augustina told him. She'd already guessed who her visitor was. Even though Stilton had been her faithful secretary for more than twenty years, he'd never once managed to recognize Grandpa John. And sure enough, a moment later Stilton showed Grandpa John in.

"I didn't expect to see you this morning, John. What a lovely surprise. Have you come to take me to lunch?"

"Hmph!" Salzburg said from her shoulder. She'd been hoping Grandmama Julietta Augustina would take her to Filbert's Fine Grocery Store on her lunch hour and buy her fresh pineapple.

"No. Not today. I have a favor I need to ask of you— not as your husband, but as a concerned citizen."

"A favor? What kind of favor?"

"I need to borrow the music box from the model of the bell tower addition."

"What on earth for?"

"It's complicated, but let me try to explain. Did

you know that Captain Rojo Herring plays the violin? And quite well, too."

"Now, John, you know I don't concern myself with the hobbies of pirates."

"Well, it got me thinking about beautiful music and its unintended side effects on people, and . . . well, other things, too. Captain Rojo Herring was down at the lake the other night playing his violin, and his music was so beautiful. And then something amazing, and well, amazingly worrisome happened—"

"What does any of this have to do with the music box?" Grandmama asked, interrupting him.

"Maybe nothing. But I need to borrow the music box to do an experiment. If I'm right then—"

"An experiment? You mean like a science experiment?"

"No, that's not what I'm saying—"

"Because Dr. Presnelda will have a fit if you enter this science experiment of yours in the science fair. What if you won? I can't imagine what she'd do if someone other than one of her students took first place."

Grandmama chuckled as she pictured Dr. Presnelda's distress at losing. Grandpa sighed and wished he were the sort of person other people listened to without interrupting.

"Julietta," he said firmly. "This isn't about Dr. Presnelda. This is about Lucky and the bell tower."

"Lucky? What on earth does Lucky have to do with the bell tower?"

Grandpa opened his mouth to explain, but this time he was interrupted by a knock at the door. Stilton peeked in.

"Mayor Chu is on the phone for you," he said.

"Tell her I'll call her back."

"She's called your office five times already today. She's insisting I put her call through."

"I'd better take this," Grandmama told Grandpa as she picked up her phone. "Then I promise I'll give you my full attention."

"Julietta Augustina, I have some news for you," Kate Chu barked into the phone.

"Good news, I hope."

"It's good news for me. I wanted you to be the first to know that after a great deal of effort I've finally managed to acquire a truly qualified dentist for the citizens of Munch."

"Interesting," Grandmama said, even though she

had no idea why Mayor Chu thought this piece of information would be interesting to anyone. "Now if you don't mind, I'm a little busy at the moment discussing an important matter with a constituent."

She gave Grandpa a smile, realizing as she did so that she'd completely forgotten why he'd come to see her.

"The dentist's name is Dr. Christobel Pike," Mayor Chu continued. "As I'm sure you know, she comes highly recommended."

"What! You can't steal our dentist! You wouldn't dare!"

"Now, now," Mayor Chu said. "No need to get upset. I'm happy to let you keep her provided that you do one small thing."

"I wouldn't bargain with you if you'd stolen the last dentist on earth!"

"Now hear me out. All I need is for you to admit—in writing—that Munch's Generic Jelly is superior in every way to that pale, tasteless organic jam you make in your town."

"Never!"

"Oh, dear. I had hoped we could work together here. But never mind. We know our jelly is better.

And it only makes sense that the town that produces the best jelly should also have the best dentist."

"Now you listen here, Kate," Grandmama yelled into the phone, but Mayor Chu had already hung up.

"How dare she!" Grandmama said, giving Grandpa John a wild-eyed stare. "Stilton? Stilton! Bring my coat. We're going to visit Dr. Pike!"

And with that, she stormed out of her office, leaving Grandpa John alone with his concerns about Lucky.

After School

After school that day, Anderson Brigby Bright Doe III offered to walk Lucinda Wilhelmina Hinojosa home.

"Do I know you?" Lucinda asked.

"I'm Anderson Brigby Bright," he said. "Anderson Brigby Bright Doe III. I'm taking you to the Science Fair Dance."

Lucinda squinted at him through her small chic glasses, then shrugged.

"Hmmmm," she hummed. "If you say so."

"I was thinking that perhaps I could carry your books for you. It's old-fashioned, I know, but doesn't it sound romantic?"

"Not really," Lucinda said. "And I don't need you to carry my books. I have my wagon with me. I'll just put them in there."

"We could go on the trail that leads past Lake Remarkable, which is also quite romantic," Anderson Brigby Bright persisted. "And while we're there, perhaps I could paint a portrait of you sitting on a rock."

"Why would you want to do that?"

"What do you mean why?" The question unsettled Anderson Brigby Bright. He'd never thought about why he wanted to paint before. "Because I'm good at it, of course."

"Mmm-hmmm," Lucinda said. "But I can't be bothered with that kind of thing today. I have to check on the progress of the bell tower. I hear it's nearly finished."

"Well, how about I go with you and walk you home afterward?" Anderson Brigby Bright thought this was a gallant offer on his part, since his time was better spent painting. True love, he knew, sometimes required great sacrifice.

Lucinda, unfortunately, didn't seem to appreciate his gesture. "If the bell tower is nearly done, then I have to finish getting these milk cartons delivered. I don't have any time to waste."

"How could posing for a portrait be a waste of time?" Anderson Brigby Bright asked, utterly astonished. But he was talking to Lucinda's back. She had already walked away, humming as she pulled her red wagon behind her.

"Hmmm-mmmm-mmmm," Lucinda Wilhelmina Hinojosa hummed to herself as she and her red wagon rattled into downtown Remarkable. "Hmmm-mmm-mmm-mm-mmmm-mm."

She took a deep breath so she could hum some more, but found herself choking instead. The air was thick with the stinkiest stench she'd ever come across. It smelled like rotten eggs, moldy boots, dead hamsters, and wilted flowers.

She glanced back nervously at her milk cartons. It was possible that the smell was coming from the milk inside. This wouldn't be surprising since she'd left her red wagon out in the hot sun while she was at school. But while it was true that the milk in the cartons had gone off, the vile smell happened to be coming from Jeb, Ebb, and Flotsam.

"You there, little girl," Flotsam called as he hurried to catch up with her. "Where'd you learn that sea chantey you be humming?" He stepped in front of her to stop her from walking away, and Ebb stood behind her to keep her from fleeing in the direction she'd come.

"It is not a sea chantey," Lucinda said huffily as she pushed past him. "It's a song by a very famous composer."

"We're looking for someone who used to sing a song kind o' like that one," Flotsam told her, stepping in front of her again. "And we think ye might know somethin' of 'is whereabouts. He be a pirate captain by the name of—"

"Why should I care?" Lucinda interrupted. "I have my own missing person to look for. Here." She shoved a milk carton into Flotsam's hand. "Do you recognize that man?"

"No."

"Well, you should. He's Ysquibel, the most influential living musician in the world today. Is the person you're looking for famous or influential?"

"Well . . . not exactly, I suppose. He warn't even a very good pirate."

"Then you might as well let him stay lost," she told them firmly. And before they could say another word, she pushed past Flotsam again and headed off to the bell tower.

Flotsam and Ebb watched her go, while Jeb sniffed at the milk carton.

"Garrhh!" he said. "This milk be as sour as old socks."

"What business be it of yours if that girl wants to pass out sour milk."

"Because I'm starving!" Jeb growled fiercely, and his stomach growled fiercely, too. "We ain't had nuthin' to eat in days but ice cream!" Jeb tended to get angry when he was hungry—a condition known as "being hangry."

"We don't eat until we finds our Captain Rojo Herring," Flotsam said firmly.

"And I say we eat now or I bust both o' yer noses!" Jeb snarled. It was a persuasive argument, and Ebb and Flotsam followed him meekly as he stormed off into the nearest restaurant.

Jeb, Ebb, and Flotsam had not spent much time on land, but in their limited experience, they'd come to understand that business owners were usually appalled and unnerved to discover they had pirates for customers. They didn't mind this, of course, because pirates enjoy being unnerving and appalling.

But they themselves were unnerved and appalled when they walked into Remarkable's House of

Otherworldly Pizza. Madame Yvette Gladiola not only didn't seem to mind pirates, she even appeared to have been expecting them.

"We wants some food and we wants it now," Jeb growled at her as he smashed his fist on the table.

Madame Gladiola didn't so much as flinch. "Of course you do. I have foreseen it. Your pizza is just coming out of the oven."

"What do ye mean? We hain't even ordered yet," Ebb said. "How do you know you made us the kind o' pizza we like?"

"I know all and I see all, of course. You want a super deluxe supreme with extra artichoke hearts, a double serving of anchovies, and no onions."

"But I love onions," Jeb snarled.

"I'm sure you do. But I have also foreseen that eating onions will give you a tummy ache that will keep you up half the night."

"Oh, right. I forgot that onions don't always agree with me innards."

While they were speaking, Flotsam sat down at the table and studied the milk carton that Lucinda had given them.

"This ain't such a bad idea. We could get our own milk cartons to hand out."

"And where do ye propose we get a good photo of our fine captain?" Ebb asked. "Since he be so miserably camera-shy."

"We don't need a stinking picture," Flotsam said. "This 'ere missing musician looks a fair bit like him. Alls we needs to do is steal them milk cartons from that young lassie and then draw a mustache and pirate hat on his wicked mug."

"Pah!" Madame Gladiola said as she brought the pizza over to the table. "Those worthless milk cartons."

"And what be wrong with milk cartons?"

"Milk cartons do not know all and see all. Milk cartons cannot foretell the future. The Save Ysquibel Now! Club could have spent its money much more wisely, if you ask me."

"How's that?"

"They should have hired a psychic—one with great powers and tremendous talent. And if you're sincere about finding your captain, you will heed my advice."

"Why should we be listenin' to the likes o' you?" Flotsam grumbled.

"Because I am the greatest and most talented psychic in the world," Madame Gladiola informed him. "And if you cross my palm with silver, I shall reveal all."

* * * *

When Madame Gladiola divined the future, she did not use a crystal ball. Instead, she rubbed her shiniest pizza pan with a thin coat of olive oil and looked deeply into its reflective surface.

"Are ye sure ye know what ye be doing?" Ebb asked her. "A pizza pan seems too ordinary to—"

"Shhh," Madame Gladiola told him. "I will not be able to glimpse your destinies if you doubt my talents."

She stared at the pizza pan again and began speaking in an unearthly voice.

"O mighty spirits," she intoned, "we call on you to give answers to those who seek them. We call on you to help these three fine gentlemen find the pirate captain they seek."

The pizza parlor was filled with silence.

"It ain't working," Flotsam said grumpily. He was starting to think this was the worst idea they'd had since trusting Captain Rojo Herring when he said he was going on a short walk and would be right back.

"Perhaps the spirits need more encouragement. Perhaps if you could explain why it's so important for you to find your captain, the spirits will take pity on you."

"Bah," Flotsam said rudely. But Jeb took her request seriously.

"Life on board our ship was all pleasantlike with that captain o' ours. We ne'er had to work too hard."

"And we didn't 'ave to follow orders unless we felt like it," Ebb added. "It ain't always like that, you know. With most captains, it's all 'hoist this, swab that!' And if ye don't do it all johnny-snaplike, they'll crack you like a clamshell."

"And then some o' the captains be worse than that, even," Flotsam admitted grudgingly. "Some o' them expect ye to work from dusk 'til dawn and would feed you to the sharks if ye gave 'em any lip about it. But not the one we 'ad. With that captain, we always 'ad lots o' time to sunbathe, play shuffleboard, and make fizzy drinks with plenty o' ice and little paper umbrellies."

The candles on the tables of the restaurant flickered once, twice, and then three times. It might have been a gentle breeze, or it might have been something else.

"The spirits have heard you." Madame Gladiola told them. "They are now ready to speak."

The pirates and the psychic joined hands in a circle around the table. Madame Gladiola peered into the pizza pan.

"Reveal to us, o mighty spirits, how destiny shall deal with these three sailors as they search for what they have lost."

Her eyes rolled back into her head as she went into a trance. She muttered, "Ah-ha, I see, it is preordained then," in an eerie whisper as she rocked back and forth in her chair.

The candles flickered once more, then their flames all went out. Madame Gladiola unrolled her eyes and looked at the three pirates.

"The answers you seek have come to me—even though I do not entirely understand them."

"Wot's that supposed to mean?" Flotsam demanded.

"I have foreseen that you will not need to trouble yourself anymore with your search. Even as we speak, a mighty captain is taking the first steps toward finding you."

"Mighty? That be overstating things a bit."

"I also see visions of a clock, or maybe a watch. And the number three. Does this mean anything to you?"

"Can't say that it does. But maybe it just means that Captain Rojo Herring will find us at three o'clock some fine afternoon."

"Captain Rojo Herring?" Madame Gladiola asked. "Who is Captain Rojo Herring?"

"He be the man we paid you to find for us," Flotsam said. "He be our captain."

"Ah," she said. "Perhaps you should have been more clear with me. The spirits did not tell me of a man named Rojo Herring. They spoke only of the captain who seeks you—and that captain goes by the name of Mad Captain Penzing the Horrific."

Jeb, Ebb, and Flotsam all froze.

"Who did ye say was looking for us?" Flotsam squeaked.

"Mad Captain Penzing the Hor—"

"Don't say that name again!" Ebb shouted. "It be worse luck than all the curses of the seas to say that name out loud."

"That may be so," Madame Gladiola said calmly, "but the spirits do not lie about fate."

"Can ye talk to 'em again?" Jeb begged. "Can ye ask 'em to change their minds?"

Madame Gladiola shook her head. "You can't change fate. You can only accept it," she said.

Then a horrible mewling howl filled the air. It was a sound miserable enough to shiver anyone's timbers.

"It be too late!" Flotsam cried. "*The Wild Three O'Clock* is a-comin' for us. We all be doomed!"

A Disharmony in the Daylight

"Ahhhweeeescreeekharooo!"

The eerie, unnerving, miserable howling noise continued for several hours that afternoon.

Jane first heard it as she was leaving Wembly's Superior Drugstore. She had agreed to go buy a gallon of hydrogen peroxide and five packages of extra-wide milkshake straws as a favor for the Grimlet twins.

"We wouldn't ask you if we weren't absolutely desperate," Eddie had said. "But we can't finish the weather machine without those things, and Mr. Wembly has banned us from his store for life."

"We could break in tonight and steal the items

from him, but I'd like to think that type of petty lar-
ceny is beneath us," Melissa added.

Given that she was saving his drugstore from a
break-in, Jane felt that Mr. Wembly could have been
nicer to her when she went to pay for her purchases.
But he made her wait while he changed the tape in
the cash register and then made her wait some more
while he talked to Mr. Charles P. Comforte-Thorpe,
the poet laureate of Remarkable, about anti-itch
power.

Jane was feeling cross and bothered by the time she
left the store, and her mood wasn't improved when
the horrible howling assailed her ears.

"*Owwehoewwweyedooohlurveyoooooohhhh!*"

The sound was so bad that Jane assumed that the
Grimlet twins were somehow responsible. But when
she ran back to the secluded spot in the park where
they were waiting for her, she could see that they were
just as puzzled by the howling as she was.

"*Yewwwwaresooohtrewwwtooomeeee!*"

"That's the worst noise I've heard in years," Melissa
said admiringly.

"You mean you're not the ones making it?" Jane
asked.

"Don't I wish," Eddie said, his mind awhirl with all of the wicked cacophonous schemes he could launch, if only he could harness the powers of such a foul sound.

"Well, if it's not you, then who's doing it?" Jane asked.

The Grimlet twins shrugged. On another day, they might have been interested in finding out. Today, however, was devoted to their weather machine.

If Jane had been at home instead of at the park, she wouldn't have needed to ask the Grimlet twins about the source of the sound. She would have discovered that the horrible howling was coming from her very own backyard. More specifically, it was coming out of the mouth of her very own brother.

Although Anderson Brigby Bright Doe III wasn't going to admit it, he'd been shaken by the fact that Lucinda Wilhelmina Hinojosa wasn't interested in having her portrait painted by him. This had forced him to come to the shocking realization that maybe Jane had a point. While he was certain that deep down, Lucinda loved photorealistic painting as much as he did, he could see that perhaps she might also enjoy being serenaded by him at the dance with a beautiful song he'd written especially for her.

He didn't know much about singing, but then, he figured he didn't need to know much. All you had to do was open your mouth and let music come out. It couldn't possibly be as difficult as painting photorealistically. He closed his eyes, pictured Lucinda Wilhelmina Hinojosa's beautiful face in his mind, and began to sing a major scale, the one that usually went do re mi fa so la ti do.

"Laooowageeehhheoooo!" he sang. It sounded all right to him, so he sang it again, only this time a little louder. *"Largeekumringfrunkdoeurgog."*

It was just as he suspected. There was nothing hard about singing at all. He opened his mouth wide and prepared to sing as loudly as he possibly could.

"LURGLEEEGGFRUNK . . ." he began, but this time he was interrupted by his father, who threw open the window of his study and leaned out to shout at him.

"Anderson Brigby Bright Doe III," yelled Anderson Brigby Bright Doe II, "I told you not to yowl in the yard when I'm trying to work."

"I'm not yowling, Dad. I'm singing," Anderson

Brigby Bright said, wondering why his father was in such a bad mood.

"No, you're not," his father shouted. "You sound like a drowning duck. And you've made me lose my train of thought. Do you know how much trouble I'll get in if your mother finds out I've lost something else?"

Anderson Brigby Bright waited until his father slammed his window shut before starting to sing again. He didn't think for a moment that there was anything wrong with his voice. His father was a genius, and like many geniuses, he was often unreasonably sensitive to distraction.

"Dew new rawrg leek . . ." Anderson Brigby Bright sang, but this time he was nearly knocked down by Mrs. Zenforia Devorah Ffyfe-Smithington, who'd come running over from her house next door carrying a large, red backpack full of first-aid supplies for wild animals.

"Where is it?" she asked. "I thought I heard it howling in your yard."

"What are you talking about, Mrs. Ffyfe-Smithington?" Anderson Brigby Bright asked.

"I heard a endangered black rhino yowling in

pain," she said. "It sounded to me like the poor thing has laryngitis." Mrs. Zenforia Devorah Ffyfe-Smithington was an expert on endangered animals and spent most of her vacations traveling to faraway places so that she could rescue them from whatever was causing them to become endangered in the first place.

"There are no black rhinos here," Anderson Brigby Bright assured her.

Mrs. Zenforia Devorah Ffyfe-Smithington vaulted over the fence to continue her search. As soon as she was gone, he opened his mouth and began to sing a love song he remembered hearing on the radio once.

"*O ahhh lurve yew annnnd yeeeew lurve meeeeh toooo!*" he sang. Really, he thought to himself, there was nothing to this singing business. But then his thoughts and his singing were interrupted by the sound of giggling. He looked up to see that Penelope Hope Adelaide Catalina had come out onto the porch. She was laughing at him as she scribbled down a math equation on a notebook in her lap.

"What are you doing?" he asked, irritated at yet another interruption. Penelope Hope held up her notebook. The equation she was working on was the kind that not only had numbers, but also had Greek letters, squiggly lines, and weird little symbols all over it.

"I'm trying to calculate just how off-key your voice is," she said. "It's going to be a very large number."

"Hmph!" Anderson Brigby Bright Doe III said. She was just jealous that he'd found something else to be so very good at. Still, he didn't see why he should stand around and let her make fun of him, so he strode past her and stomped into the house with all the dignity of a maestro.

A Little Night Music

That night, after everyone else had gone to bed, Grandpa John sat at the edge of Lake Remarkable with a packet of figgy doodles on his lap. He had the small music box he'd taken from Grandmama Julietta Augustina's office next to him. Carefully, he lifted the lid and let the beautiful little tune play in the night. Then he stared out at the water and waited.

After the misery of Anderson Brigby Bright's singing that afternoon, the music sounded lovelier than ever. It took only a few moments before Grandpa saw the familiar ripple of water and then the familiar shape of Lucky as she emerged from the depths.

"Ah-hoooo," called the lake monster eagerly as she swam to where Grandpa was seated.

"Hello, old friend," Grandpa said. He pulled a figgy doodle out of the packet and tossed it to her, but Lucky ignored it. She'd begun to sway and twist in the water in time to the music. The neglected cookie sank into the lake, and Grandpa carefully closed the music box.

Lucky paused mid-sway as the music stopped. Grandpa tossed her another figgy doodle, and this time she caught it in midair and gobbled it up.

"Want another one, girl?"

Grandpa reached back into the figgy doodle packet, but as he did so, Lucky darted forward and flipped up the lid of the music box with her nose.

The music started playing again. Lucky reared up again to her full height and started dancing in the lake waters. She dipped and swirled, then moved through a series of lake monster pirouettes.

"Lucky!" Grandpa said sternly. "Stop that! Someone's going to see you." He closed the music box again and put it in his coat pocket before Lucky could reopen it. Lucky snorted at him—a very pouty and disappointed kind of snort—then dove back down into Lake Remarkable's depths.

Grandpa John stared after her worriedly. He'd been keeping an eye on Lucky for a long time now, and her health and well-being were of the utmost importance to him. It was a fact he might have shared with a few people he trusted, if any of those people had ever bothered to ask him.

He'd seen Lucky for the first time very shortly after he'd married Julietta Augustina. He'd gone for a walk by himself on a quiet night, and had stopped off at the lake just as the moon was setting and the sky was full of shooting stars. It was possible that Lucky didn't notice him, or maybe she simply sensed he was a gentle soul, but either way, she'd surfaced from the lake just as if no one were there. Grandpa John stood quietly on the shore and watched her swim in the moonlight until she hooted softly.

"Ah-hoo," came the noise across the water.

And then, for no reason he could explain later, Grandpa put his hands to his mouth and hooted back at her.

"Ah-hoo."

Lucky glided around in the water until she was facing him, gave him a long, but not unfriendly look, and then dove back down into the lake.

Grandpa John went down to Lake Remarkable every night after that, hoping to see her again, but he had no luck for several weeks. Then, on one evening that was particularly still and windless, he saw her stick her head out of the water and look around. He hooted gently at her, and this time she glided over to where he was standing. She swam, and splashed, and played in the water in front of him for nearly an hour before the sound of a car backfiring in town made her dive safely down.

Over the years, Grandpa John had learned all sorts of things about Lucky. He knew, for instance, that she wasn't purple—as most people believed—but rather a very dark turquoise. She had a short black snout and orange eyes that were surprisingly sweet. He'd discovered that her hearing was quite sensitive. Loud noises bothered her tremendously. He'd also learned that Lucky was particularly fond of figgy doodles, so he always made sure he brought some with him when he came down to the lake to visit her.

Today was the first time he'd ever seen her refuse one. She seemed to love beautiful music even more than she loved figgy doodles—and this was possibly going to be a serious problem. If she was willing to

surface to hear Ysquibel's composition on a tinny
music box, would she be able to resist it when it was
played every day at noon by fifty-seven perfectly
tuned brass bells? And if she came out of hiding in
broad daylight, she'd be spotted instantly. Grandpa
didn't like to think about what would happen next.

It didn't matter how much the people of Remarkable wanted their new bell tower. Grandpa John knew
it couldn't be allowed to chime even once. And he
knew that he'd take whatever steps were necessary to
see that it never did.

Captain Schnabel

Over the course of the next few days, Ms. Schnabel changed. She changed so much that people walking down the streets of Remarkable hardly recognized her when she passed. It wasn't just because her face was lively and smiling now, and had lost all signs of the glum expression she usually wore. And it wasn't just because she'd started striding around town with her head held up high and a rebellious look in her eye. It wasn't even that Ms. Schnabel had suddenly quit talking like a schoolteacher and had started saying things like "avast," "begad," and "savvy" when she did her everyday errands, like shopping for groceries or ordering new checks at Remarkable's Savings and Loan.

The reason that most people didn't recognize Ms. Schnabel was because she'd started dressing like a pirate captain. Instead of wearing her usual drab sweater sets and modest skirts, she wore cropped pants, a ruffled shirt, a bright silk sash, and a swashbuckling hat that was even larger than the one Captain Rojo Herring wore. Instead of wearing prim and sensibly heeled shoes, she'd taken to wearing a large pair of grimy black pirate boots with sterling silver buckles. And while pirate clothes usually look silly on people, no one could say that the outfit didn't somehow suit Ms. Schnabel perfectly.

On her first day of teaching piracy, she nearly gave Mrs. Peabody a heart attack when she ducked into the Colossal Ice Cream Palace on the way to school.

"Look now, this establishment is not some kind of pirate hangout. You and your friends can't keep showing up here and expecting me to serve you ice cream."

"I won't be requiring yer confections," Ms. Schnabel told her in an extra-snarly voice. "I just ducked in 'ere for a moment to avoid a certain half-masted blubbermouth."

Mrs. Peabody looked out the window. The only person she saw on the street was Dr. Presnelda, who was in her car waiting for the stoplight at the corner to change from red to green. This only confirmed her suspicions that all pirates were liars, since there was no good reason that anyone would want to avoid Dr. Presnelda.

"Now look here," Mrs. Peabody started to say, but she choked on whatever she was going to say next as she recognized Ms. Schnabel. "Good heavens, Delilah, why on earth are you dressed like that?"

"None of yer nevermind," Ms. Schnabel growled at her. She couldn't have cared less if Mrs. Peabody didn't approve of how she was dressed. She was on her way to school, and for the first time in her entire career as an educator, she was looking forward to getting there. If her students wanted to learn to be pirates, then begads, she would teach them a thing or two.

Jane had not really expected Ms. Schnabel to keep her promise about teaching pirate lessons. She figured after a good night's sleep, Ms. Schnabel would see what a crazy idea it was and tell the Grimlet twins that she was going back to teaching the kind of ordinary things that fifth graders learn about, like state capitals and the names of all the presidents.

But Jane had underestimated Ms. Schnabel. When she arrived at school the next morning, Jane found that the fifth-grade classroom had been transformed. Ms. Schnabel's desk was missing and had been replaced by a captain's wheel. A large skull and crossbones had been painted on the front blackboard. The bulletin board with its multiplication tables was gone, and hanging in its place were hooks for anchors, sailing rigs, and mooring lines. The industrial school carpet had been pulled out, and rough wooden slats now covered the floor. Most ominously, a heavy wooden plank extended out of one of the windows, and a sign on it read ALL WHO DISAPPOINT THE CAPTAIN SHALL WALK TO THEIR DOOM.

"Um . . . um . . . good morning, Ms. Schnabel," Jane said as she looked around the classroom.

"That be Captain Schnabel to you, you young spog," Ms. Schnabel bellowed back at her. "Spog" was a pirate term for a new recruit, which was one of many things that Jane would learn about pirates in the next few days.

Despite what Ms. Schnabel had said, training to be a pirate was not easy. Jane had to learn about seafaring knots, basic ship construction and maintenance, sword fighting, knife fighting, pirate-speak, and semaphores. She had to learn common conversion rates for pieces of eight, Spanish doubloons, and the Aztec oro. There were classes in sail hoisting, pirate vocabulary tests, and exams on maritime law. Lunch was no longer the sandwiches, chips, and juice boxes that Jane was used to bringing from home, but rather hardtack, moldy oranges, and dried seaweed.

But if Jane wasn't finding pirate lessons easy, the Grimlet twins were having a worse time of it. Ms. Schnabel the teacher might have put up with their shenanigans, but Captain Schnabel the pirate had no patience for them whatsoever. Every time they so much as looked at The Book of Dangerous Deeds and Dastardly Intentions, Captain Schnabel would immediately shout, "Unhand that, you blaggards!" and then promptly issue a punishment. Jane sometimes thought the Grimlet twins spent more time walking the plank than they did sitting at their desks. And when they weren't walking the plank, they were swabbing the classroom floor, shining the buckles on Ms. Schnabel's smelly pirate boots, or eating an extra helping of dried squid.

Jane had gotten into trouble a few times herself.

It wasn't something that usually happened, because Jane didn't usually do anything interesting enough to deserve punishment. But now Ms. Schnabel was impossible to please.

"Captain Schnabel," Jane had asked one day, "may I please go to the bathroom?" Jane's hands were covered in sticky black tar from waterproofing a fishing net, and she wanted to wash them off.

"Gar!" Captain Schnabel answered. "Use the proper pirate term, landlubber."

"May I please be excused so I can go to the . . . uh . . . poop deck?"

"Incorrect!" shouted Captain Schnabel. "The poop deck be the aftmost deck on the ship, near the captain's quarters. The term you should have been using is the *jardin* or *head*. Now, go walk the plank to see if it helps your memory for the next time."

Jane sighed, but it could have been worse. If she'd been on a real pirate ship, she would have had to walk down a board and jump into the shark-infested ocean. At school, however, the plank only led out a first-story window, and once Jane dropped off of it, she'd land in a small wading pool full of water. For the rest of the day, she'd have to feel her damp socks squishing around in her wet shoes, which wasn't very pleasant, but was still much better than being eaten by sharks.

There wasn't much point in complaining, however, because whenever Jane or either of the Grimlet twins complained, Captain Schnabel would simply remind them that they'd all agreed to abide by the Code of the Pirates, which was a set of rules and regulations that governed pirate life. A copy of it was posted by the captain's wheel at the front of the classroom. It had been one of the first things Captain Schnabel had taught them about piracy.

"Today we are going to discuss the Code of the Pirates," Captain Schnabel had said. "Now, who here can tell me what that is?"

No one could, of course, since it was their first pirate lesson, but this displeased Captain Schnabel, so she made each of them walk the plank once before letting them sit down in their seats again.

"The Code of the Pirates," Captain Schnabel explained, "is an agreement between the captain of a pirate ship, in this case me, and the crew, which would be you three. The code sets forth the rules under which the ship will be governed."

"What happens if we break one of the rules?" Eddie asked eagerly.

"You cannot break the rules. It isn't allowed under the code."

"But what happens if one gets broken anyway—say by accident."

"Are you planning on breaking one by accident?" Captain Schnabel asked, giving Eddie such a ferocious glower that he shook in his wet socks.

"Um. No . . . not anymore."

"Good. Now normally, the captain and the crew would come up with the terms together, but since you sorry lot didn't even know what they were in the first place, I've written them myself."

She unfurled a scroll she had tucked into the colorful silk sash wrapped around her pirate shirt and began to read.

"Number One: No breaking the Pirates' Code, for any reason. Number Two: The captain's word is law. Number Three: The crew must immediately obey all of the captain's orders. Number Four: No one can challenge the captain or lie to the captain. Number Five: A pirate only keeps promises made to other pirates. All other promises must be broken immediately.

Number Six: The crew and captain will stay together until it is mutually decided that they've accomplished the mission of the ship. Now, are there any questions?"

No one said anything. Jane and the Grimlet twins just looked at each other nervously.

"Then sign the code," Captain Schnabel said, brandishing a quill pen at them. None of her three students stood up.

"Sign the code or spend the rest of the day walking the plank!" Captain Schnabel roared. Jane and the Grimlet twins signed. They didn't have much choice.

"I can't help but feel that somehow our plan has backfired," Eddie said glumly as he, Melissa, and Jane walked out of the public school. Their arms were full of fishing nets, compasses, spyglasses, cutlasses, maps of the ocean, and all of the other pirate gear that Captain Schnabel had given them as part of their homework.

"Who'd have guessed she'd be so enthusiastic about it?" Melissa grumbled. "Life was easier when we had nothing to do at school but cause trouble."

"Do you guys want to go to the library with me and get started on our pirate book reports?" Jane asked.

"We can't," Melissa told her. "We need to get our

weather machine ready by Friday, and I don't see how we're going to manage it with all this homework she's given us."

"But the science fair doesn't start until Saturday," Jane said. "The only thing happening on Friday is the Science Fair Dance."

"Oh, is that right?" Eddie was doing his best to sound innocent.

"What are you two planning?" Jane asked suspiciously. She'd been hanging around the Grimlet twins long enough to know that the only time they sounded innocent was when they were up to no good.

"Nothing," Melissa said. "Nothing at all. And on the off chance we were planning something, wouldn't you rather not know?"

She had a point, but before Jane could answer, Anderson Brigby Bright Doe III came running around the street corner.

"Jane! Jane! I've been looking for you everywhere!" he cried. "I need to ask you something."

"What is it?" Jane asked, feeling more suspicious of her brother than she had of the Grimlet twins.

"I can't speak about it in front of other people. I need to talk to you in private."

"Right now?" Jane said. She and the Grimlet twins had walked all the way to the front of their creepy black house. As usual, Jane had been hoping that they would remember to invite her inside and introduce her to their notorious bank-robbing parents. But as usual, the Grimlet twins pushed and shoved each other down the broken front sidewalk and then disappeared behind the crooked front door without so much as saying good-bye.

"Jane," Anderson Brigby Bright said. "You're the only one I can trust. You're the only one in town who knows anything about mediocrity!"

It was the closest that Anderson Brigby Bright had ever come to saying she had any abilities worth noticing. Jane tried her best not to feel flattered.

"What did you want to ask me?" Jane said. But Anderson Brigby Bright hadn't waited for her. He was already running in the direction of the gifted school. Jane sighed and ran after him.

Mediocrity

Remarkable's School for the Remarkably Gifted was located at the top of Mount Magnificent, which was slightly shorter than Remarkable Hill, but much steeper. But as Anderson Brigby Bright approached the school's parking lot, he suddenly veered into the woods and down a small road not often taken.

"Anderson Brigby Bright! Where are you going?" Jane called as she followed him.

"We'll be there soon," he called back. A moment later he veered off the road not often taken and onto a trail nobody bothered with.

"I'm getting tired." She was still carrying her pirate gear from school, and it was quite heavy.

"Quit complaining. We're here," Anderson Brigby Bright said. He'd stopped in a small clearing in the middle of the forest. "It's the most secluded spot in all of Remarkable. I want to be sure we aren't overheard."

"Why?" Jane said wearily as she dumped her pirate homework on the ground.

"I need your advice, Jane," he said despairingly. "My problem is that I had a brilliant idea."

"Okay," Jane said, not understanding how this would be a problem.

"I decided to woo Lucinda Wilhelmina Hinojosa with a song, since she likes music so much. That's brilliant, right?"

Jane gave him a dark look. "It was my idea, remember? I suggested it to you at dinner."

Anderson Brigby Bright looked confused for a moment. "I don't remember that." Then he brightened. "But if it really was your idea, that probably explains why it isn't working. Jane, it's possible . . . just possible that I am not excellent at singing."

"So?" Jane said.

"So? So I've always been good at everything I've tried. I don't know how to be bad at something. That's why I came to you."

"But, Anderson Brigby Bright, the only thing you've ever tried to do is paint photorealistically . . ."

"That's not the point. The point is that I can't fail. I need you to listen to me sing."

"Do I have to?" Jane protested. But Anderson Brigby Bright had already opened his mouth and started to . . . well, Jane wouldn't have called it singing. It was more annoying than that. It was more horrible than the sound the Grimlet twins made when they were making raspberries with their armpits. It was more irritating than the rash Jane got when Melissa accidentally dropped one of Eddie's experimental homemade itch bombs. Anderson Brigby Bright only sang for a few moments, but it was the longest few moments Jane could ever remember living through.

"Well?" he said. His face was full of hope as he waited for her to give him some good news.

"Um." Jane tried to be diplomatic about it. "It's not the best singing I've ever heard."

"But it's not the worst, either. Right?"

"I didn't exactly say that."

"But I'm good at everything I do," Anderson Brigby Bright said, stomping his foot a little, as if this would change Jane's mind.

From above them, up in one of the trees, came the sound of snickering. It was Penelope Hope Adelaide Catalina. She was sitting on a branch with a thick book about math in her lap.

"What are you doing up there!" Anderson Brigby Bright demanded angrily. "Did you follow me so you could spy on us?"

"Hardly," Penelope Hope said as she swung down out of the tree. "I came here to work on my differential equations. It's the most secluded spot in Remarkable, you know. I thought it would be nice to get away from your caterwauling for a while."

"It's not caterwauling!" Anderson Brigby Bright shouted at her. "And I'm getting better. The only thing I need is more practice without all this criticism."

"Anderson Brigby Bright, sometimes no amount of practice will make up for a genuine lack of talent," Jane said gently. It was something that she knew better than anyone. But Anderson Brigby Bright didn't want to listen to her.

"You just feel that way because you're you," Anderson Brigby Bright said. "I'm me. Singing isn't hard. I know I can learn to do this."

"You might try attempting something easier to impress Lucinda," Penelope Hope suggested with as straight a face as she could manage.

"Like what?"

"Like locating Ysquibel." She started laughing again. "You're probably at least as good at finding people as you are at singing."

"I could find Ysquibel if I wanted to!" Anderson Brigby Bright shouted. "It would be easy for someone like me. I'm right, aren't I, Jane. Jane?"

He looked around, but Jane was nowhere to be seen. She'd had the good sense to slip out of the clearing before she had to answer him.

Crisis at the Library

While Penelope Hope and Anderson Brigby Bright continued their argument about whether he had the skill set to find the world's most famous missing musician (if such an activity was worth his time, which it almost certainly wasn't), Jane headed off to the library to find a book for her book report.

As you might imagine, Remarkable had one of the finest public libraries in the world. Millicent Margaret VanderTweed, the head reference librarian, had always believed that the library's collection had one or more books on every worthwhile topic under the sun. But on this day, she found that her faith was being tested.

"How do you spell his name again?" she asked Jane.

"R-O-J-O space H-E-R-R-I-N-G," Jane answered.

"And he's a pirate captain, you say?"

"Yes. I'm supposed to do a report on a legendary pirate for school. I chose him because he just moved to town and is very nice."

Ms. VanderTweed typed his name into the library's computer again—then tried alternate spellings, like *Roho Hairring* and *Rouxhoux Herhing*. The computer still produced no results.

"It's just so odd . . ." she muttered to herself as she went into the book stacks to the pirate section. By the time Jane caught up with her, she was atop a long, rolling bookshelf ladder, reading the titles of books on one of the high shelves in the nonfiction section.

"You are absolutely certain that Captain Rojo Herring exists? Because if he existed, we'd have a book on him."

"I'm very sure he exists," Jane said. "I've been to his house. He lives in the Mansion at the Top of Remarkable Hill."

"I don't suppose I could interest you in a book about the mansion instead. We have several interesting histories about the ghosts that inhabit it . . . one of the ghosts is called The Gruel. Apparently it wanders the hallways as a lumpy, oatmeal-like apparition.

And don't even get me started on the Vicious Valkyrie."

"No, thanks," Jane said. "Ms. Schnabel would never accept a book report about ghosts."

Ms. VanderTweed sighed and climbed down from the ladder.

"It's possible, I suppose, that any book we have on Captain Rojo Herring might have gotten lost in our vast section on Mad Captain Penzing the Horrific. Now there's a legendary pirate captain."

"What's he famous for?" Jane asked.

"*He's* not famous for anything. Mad Captain Penzing the Horrific is a woman. I believe her first name is Mirabel."

"I never heard of her."

"Well, you should have. She was quite famous in her day. She once captured the entire Portuguese Navy using a piece of old string and a variety of lobster baskets."

"Really?"

"And a few years back she had a school of trained sharks. No one's ever been able to train sharks before, but they were apparently so afraid of her that they'd do anything she wanted. She was the scariest thing in the ocean up until the day she disappeared."

"She disappeared? What happened to her?"

"She collected so much treasure that her pirate ship, *The Wild Three O'Clock*, sank to the bottom of the Sea of Cortez," Ms. VanderTweed said as she pulled a thick book off the shelf. "She was then captured and sent to prison in the port town of Ferragudo."

"Is she still there?"

"Oh, heavens no," Ms. VanderTweed said. "No prison could hold Mad Captain Penzing. She demanded a trial—but no one could prove that she'd plundered anything because all of the evidence was at the bottom of the ocean. Finally, they were forced to release her to her relatives, who promised to see that she never returned to pirating."

"Wow."

"Are you sure you wouldn't rather do your report on her? There are so many excellent biographies about her life."

Jane thought about it for a moment then shook her head. Mad Captain Penzing the Horrific might be exciting, but Captain Rojo Herring was her friend.

Ms. VanderTweed sighed. "Fine. Why don't you come back tomorrow? Maybe I'll have found something on your captain by then."

* * * * *

Meanwhile, back in town, Mrs. Peabody was dealing with problems of her own.

The smelly pirates had returned to her ice cream parlor. And not only had they returned, but they were in no hurry to leave.

"We be waiting on someone," Flotsam growled at her when she tried to take their order.

"Well, you can't wait here all day. I'm going to need this table for my other customers."

Jeb and Ebb snickered to each other. Her other customers had left in a hurry shortly after they'd arrived. Mrs. Peabody glowered at them for a moment before heading to the kitchen to call Mayor Doe and file another complaint about how pirates were stinking up her restaurant.

As soon as she was gone, however, the mood at the pirates' table grew more somber.

"Where is 'e," Flotsam grumbled. He was talking about Detective Burton Sly. Several days earlier, they'd pooled their pieces of eight and hired the detective to help them.

"I'm sure he'll be 'ere in 'is own time," Ebb said soothingly.

"We don't 'ave time, though, do we? Every moment

we 'ang around 'ere puts us one moment closer to 'aving to sign our 'x' for Mad Captain Penzing the 'orrific."

"Don't say that name," Jeb said weakly.

"I have to say it. How else do I remind ye of wot happens to us if the Mad Captain find us befores we finds Captain Rojo Herring? Ye wants to be on a ship where ye be expected to work fer yer living?"

"No more sunbathing or shuffleboard," Ebb said sadly. "And no more fizzy drinks."

"And if ye don't jump to when the captain barks an order, you'll be turned into shark bait faster than you can say heave-ho."

"Can we talk about something else?" Jeb suggested.

But they did not need to come up with a new topic of conversation. Right at that moment, Detective Burton Sly slipped into the Colossal Ice Cream Palace and joined them at the table.

"Gentlemen, I apologize for my lateness," said Detective Burton Sly. He'd spent part of the day disguised as a bush and still had bits of twigs and leaves stuck in his eyebrows.

"Where be our captain?"

"I'm afraid I still don't know."

"But we 'ad a bargain. We paid you to find 'im."

"And I thought I had. I had a lead on a man with two peg legs, a big captain's hat, a green parrot—everything you described. I was convinced that this case would be closed almost as soon as I'd opened it. But I quickly discovered that this man was not the man you are looking for."

"How's that?"

"There was one small discrepancy between him and your missing captain that I was unable to resolve. The man I found was not a pirate. It was obvious to me he'd spent very little of his life at sea."

"Arghh, that be a disappointment," said Flotsam, staring at the detective menacingly. "And we don't 'ave time to deal with disappointment."

Detective Burton Sly glared back at Flotsam. He didn't like working with pirates, and he didn't like having them hanging around Remarkable. The sooner he could find their captain and send them on their way, the better.

"There is, well . . . I wouldn't call it a lead, but a certain rumor I've heard that might be of interest."

"Aye? And what be that?"

"My sources tell me that the public school is offering pirate lessons now."

"But what good be that to us," Jeb grumbled. "We already knows how to be pirates."

"Whoever is teaching these children must know an awful lot about pirating. Is it possible that your captain would take a job as a schoolteacher?"

"It'd be possible, I reckon," Ebb said. "But he wouldn't be much good at it. He barely knew his mizzenmast from his orlop deck."

"Or his poop deck from his head," snickered Flotsam.

"He were good at playing a pirate jig on his fiddle, though," Jeb reminisced. "He used to serenade us to sleep."

"I'd be willing to launch an investigation at the school yard," Detective Burton Sly said. "Do some reconnaissance, take some surveillance photos, perhaps get some police sketches made up. All for my usual fee, of course."

The three pirates conferred for a moment before turning back to the detective.

"Thank ye, but no. You be fired." Jeb told him.

"We can track him down for ourselves now. We won't be wasting any mores of yer time," said Ebb.

"And you won't be wasting any more of ours," added Flotsam. And then the three pirates walked out of the ice cream parlor, laughing their wicked pirate laughs.

Promises

The next morning Jane awoke to the sound of Anderson Brigby Bright singing in the shower. She groaned and put her pillow over her head, but it didn't matter. There was no way she could block out that horrible off-key wailing. Although it didn't seem possible, his singing was getting worse every day. Jane could only hope that Lucinda Wilhelmina Hinojosa would appreciate the thought and effort that Anderson Brigby Bright was putting into his song, and not care so much about the horribly mangled music that was produced as a result of that thought and effort.

"*Ohwwww I luuuuuvvee yeeeeeeeeew, oh yeeessssssss eye dewwwwwwww!*" Anderson Brigby Bright sang.

There was no point in trying to get any more sleep. The only thing to do was to get as far away from Anderson Brigby Bright's voice as possible. Jane got out of bed and got dressed as quickly as she could.

She decided she might as well stop by the library before school to see if Ms. VanderTweed had found anything for her on Captain Rojo Herring. Jane hadn't been at all certain that the library would be open that early in the morning, so she was pleased to discover that the big front doors were unlocked.

But the reason the doors were unlocked was because Ms. VanderTweed had never closed the library the day before. She'd been there all night doing her best to find out something about Captain Rojo Herring.

Jane found Ms. VanderTweed sitting behind the reference desk. Her hair was frazzled, her sweater set was rumpled, and her librarian glasses were askew. She glared at Jane through them.

"He's not real," Ms. VanderTweed snapped at her. "I went through every reference I could find—and it turns out you were wrong."

"What do you mean?"

"Captain Rojo Herring is not a real person. He's

fictional—nothing more than a minor character in the opera *Prise de Corsaire*." She slapped a thin manila folder down on the reference desk in front of Jane. "See for yourself."

"Um . . . okay," Jane said as she took the folder and headed over to one of the library's study carrels. Ms. VanderTweed looked so exhausted that Jane didn't have the heart to argue with her about it. Maybe someday she would bring Captain Rojo Herring in so that he could introduce himself to her.

The manila folder had only a few sheets of paper containing what little information Ms. VanderTweed had been able to find. As Jane read through them, she learned that *Prise de Corsaire* was an opera about the exploits of Mad Captain Penzing the Horrific—and that the character of Captain Rojo Herring was marooned on a desert island in the first act. More interestingly, she learned that *Prise de Corsaire* was written by none other than Ysquibel.

"Oh, wow," she said to herself. The name Captain Rojo Herring was so unusual—and she couldn't help but wonder if maybe, just maybe, Ysquibel had chosen it because he knew Captain Rojo Herring. And if he knew him, then maybe they were even friends. And if they were friends, then maybe, just maybe, Captain Rojo Herring knew where Ysquibel was.

"Oh, wow," she said to herself again. Maybe she could tell someone, and maybe that someone could use the information to find Ysquibel. "Oh, wow, oh, wow, oh, wow."

"What's that now, Jane?"

Jane nearly jumped out of her seat. Grandpa was sitting in the carrel next to her. She didn't know when he'd come in or how long he'd been there.

"Grandpa!" she said. "I didn't see you."

"Most people don't," he agreed. "I just stopped by to return a book I borrowed on the inner workings of bell towers."

"I thought you didn't like bell towers."

"I don't like them. Jane—what happened to your hands?"

Jane shrugged. Her fingers were covered in Band-Aids. "It's from rope-tying class. Captain Schnabel is teaching us how to tie seafaring knots."

"Ah, yes. Your grandmother tells me that Ms. Schnabel is teaching piracy these days."

"How did she know that?"

"Your grandmother knows almost everything that

goes on in this town. Still, I don't think even she realized that knot tying was so hazardous."

"It's probably not usually. We just don't have the right kind of rope. The one we're using is the climbing rope from the gym. Captain Schnabel cut it down with her sword. But it's old and full of splinters."

"I'd think a gym rope would be much too thick for good knot tying."

"It is. She wants us to learn how to tie a shroud knot, and an eye splice, and a chain sennit, but none of us can do it right because the rope won't bend enough. She said my double overhand knot looks more like an untied shoelace."

"It sounds like you need some better ropes."

"Sure," Jane agreed. "But Captain Schnabel says that pirates have to make do with what's on hand, because when you're off at sea, you can't run to the store every time something's not to your liking."

"I see," Grandpa said thoughtfully. "But what if you just happened to come across some lovely new ropes on your way to school this morning. Would she let you use them?"

"She might. But she'd probably prefer it if I pillaged them from somewhere. She had a lot of fun pillaging the climbing rope from the gymnasium. There was nothing Coach Dunder could do to stop her."

"And what if I leave some ropes lying around for you to pillage? Do you think you could learn to tie knots without hurting yourself then?"

"You could do that?" Jane looked at her grandpa hopefully. "It would make things so much easier."

"But you must promise me one thing—you need to keep these ropes a secret. I don't want Captain Schnabel or anyone else figuring out they came from me."

"Sure," Jane agreed, but she wasn't really paying attention. She was imagining what good knots she'd be able to tie and how pleased Captain Schnabel would be with her.

"Jane," Grandpa said sharply. "Are you sure you heard me? You must promise not to tell anyone about the ropes unless I say it's okay. Not anyone. Do you understand?"

"Yeah, Grandpa, I understand," Jane said. It seemed like an easy enough promise to keep. Jane went back to the reference desk to ask Ms. Vander-Tweed for a book about pirate knots. When she got back to her carrel, Grandpa was gone. But in his chair were several coils of brand-new, highly pliable rope.

Jane wondered how he'd managed to get them for her so quickly, but then she looked up at the library clock and realized that she needed to leave if she wanted to get to school on time. She scooped the ropes into her backpack and went on her way.

Truancy

Skipping school for no good reason is known as truancy—and in Remarkable, as in most towns, truancy is against the law. Naturally, this meant the Grimlet twins were only too delighted to give it a try. So when the school bell rang that morning, they were not in Ms. Schnabel's classroom as they should have been. Instead, they were hiding out in their secret lair, which sounded like an exciting place to be, but was actually just an unused garden shed in the backyard of their creepy black house.

"I can't believe we never thought of it before," Melissa Grimlet said as she wrote TRUANCY in big invisible letters in The Book of Dangerous Deeds and Dastardly Intentions.

"It was quite remiss of us," Eddie agreed. "High time we got around to it. I feel quite pleased."

"Me too," Melissa said. "In fact, I think I feel even more pleased than you do."

Of course, she was lying—and Eddie was lying, too. Neither one of them felt any pride in what they were doing that day. Down at the bottom of their tiny black hearts, they knew the real reason they were skipping school had nothing to do with adding another dastardly deed to their long list of dreadful accomplishments. The real reason was that they hadn't finished their pirate homework and were scared of what Captain Schnabel might do to them when she found out.

The Grimlet twins hadn't had time for homework. They'd spent every free minute on their science fair project instead—and even that hadn't been entirely successful. The weather machine still needed a lot of work. Skipping school to make sure it would be ready in time was the only sensible thing to do—even if Melissa and Eddie would have denied being sensible just as vehemently as they would have denied being scared.

"You don't think Captain Schnabel will come looking for us, do you?" Melissa asked. She tried to sound brave, but her hands were shaking just a little as she picked up the schematics for the weather machine.

Eddie gulped as he adjusted the settings on the weather machine's barometer. "I can't imagine she'd bother. She's probably so busy with her pirate captaining that she won't have even noticed that we're not there."

But of course, Ms. Schnabel had noticed. And she noticed when the Grimlet twins didn't show up on Wednesday either. By Thursday, she was quite agitated about it.

"Whar be yer scurvy friends?" she asked Jane. Jane shrugged.

"I don't know. I haven't seen them."

"What's yer best guess as to their whereabouts then? Tell me or I'll make you walk the plank again."

"Um . . ." Jane said, thinking hard. "Maybe they're off somewhere working on their science fair project."

"You mean that science fair project be real? What kind o' project is it?"

"Um . . ." Jane knew she was not supposed to tell

anyone about it, but she was pretty sure it was against the pirates' code to keep secrets from the captain. "It's a weather machine."

"A machine that controls the weather? Well burn and sink me, that'd be something. Do ye think those two scoundrels can pull it off?"

"I don't know," Jane said. "They seem to think it will work."

"Aye, if it does, they'll win for sure." Captain Schnabel flashed a grin as she thought of how much her sister would hate losing the science fair trophy to two public school students. Then her face returned to its stern, piratey scowl. "But they should give up that weather project of theirs and come back to learning the ways of the buccaneer. They could make a career out of it, they could."

"Um . . . what about me?" Jane said. "Do you think piracy would be a good career for me?"

Captain Schnabel gave Jane a thoughtful, sympathetic look.

"Jane, me deary," she said, "how can I put this all diplomatic-like? It be clear to me that you always try yer hardest—and I always say a hard-working pirate is the best kind. But not all captains are as savvy as I am. You have a certain lack of aptitude that might get yerself thrown overboard."

"Oh," Jane said. "I was hoping I might be a good pirate. Maybe good enough to be as famous as Mad Captain Penzing the Horrific."

"Mad Captain Penzing the Horrific? Where did you learn about the likes of that one?"

"In a book. I was going to do my report on Captain Rojo Herring, but the library didn't have anything on him. So I checked out a book about Mad Captain Penzing the Horrific instead."

"Bah!" Captain Schnabel said as if libraries were below contempt. "Ye don't want to wind up like Mad Captain Penzing the Horrific. Yer grandmother would never speak to ye again if ye became a pirate, for one thing. And for another, that mad captain came to a sad, sad end."

"She still got to be famous for a while," Jane said. "They have a whole section in the library about her. Grandma would be impressed with me if I had my own section in the library. And Ysquibel even wrote an opera about her."

"Bah!" Captain Schnabel said, as if opera was even more contemptible than libraries. "That's not a good enough reason. Yer not really the pirating type, young Jane, and being true to yer real self is the most important thing you can do with yer life."

"My real self? But my real self isn't good at anything."

"Yer real self is exceptional at being an ordinary girl with good intentions who loves dogs. And that be a fine thing to be. You should work hard at being that."

The dismissal bell rang. Jane started to gather up her belongings so that she could head home.

"I'll see ye in the morning, spog," Captain Schnabel said.

"See you tomorrow, Captain," Jane replied as she headed out the classroom door.

But they were both very much mistaken. The next day was going to be full of surprises—the kind of surprises that meant they would not be seeing each other again for a long, long time.

The Terrible Truth

When Jeb, Ebb, and Flotsam fired Detective Burton Sly, they not only hurt his feelings, but also his sense of self-worth. He spent three days in his darkened office, soothing his wounded pride by playing solitaire and swigging aloe vera juice from a hip flask.

On the fourth day, he reminded himself of what he'd always taught his junior detectives: Good investigators never give up, and great investigators never fail. And since he was the greatest investigator of all, he knew he had no choice but to find the missing captain, even if his clients had lost faith in him.

He spent the rest of the week observing his number

one suspect until he had obtained all of the surveillance photos, wiretaps, and hard evidence he needed to take the next step—which was to confront said suspect with his allegations.

He strode briskly from his office to the suspect's house, walked up the front steps past the potted plants, and knocked firmly on the door. A moment later, the door was opened by a woman who was entirely unfamiliar to him.

"Who are you?" he demanded.

"I am the esteemed Dr. Presnelda, head of Remarkable's School for the Remarkably Gifted," she answered with irritation. "What are you doing on my porch?"

"I'm Detective Burton Sly," he replied. "I've come on an urgent matter. I am looking for a lost pirate captain."

Dr. Presnelda went quite pale—a fact that might have been missed by a person less observant that Detective Sly. "I . . ." she said. "I don't know what you're talking about. You must have the wrong house."

She tried to shut the door in his face, but the detective put his foot across the doorjamb to keep it from closing.

"Ma'am," he said, "I do not have the wrong house. And furthermore, I sense you know something you aren't telling me."

"I don't have to talk to you!"

"That won't stop me from discovering the truth."

"You don't understand." Dr. Presnelda was trembling now. "My place in this town, my reputation as an educator—it will all be destroyed if anyone ever found out . . ."

"I can be very discreet. You have to trust me. But it is of the utmost importance that you tell me what you know of Captain Rojo Herring."

Dr. Presnelda's confusion was as genuine as her relief. "I don't know a Captain Rojo Herring. Captain Rojo Herring has nothing whatsoever to do with me."

She once again tried to close the door, and Detective Burton Sly once again stopped her with his foot.

"Perhaps it's an alias," he suggested.

"Perhaps it isn't," Dr. Presnelda snapped.

"Perhaps the best thing would be for you to let me inside so we can clear this matter up."

Dr. Presnelda led Detective Burton Sly to the living room. He slid his case file to her across the top of the coffee table. She flipped the file open and found herself looking at the image of a pirate captain taken from a great distance through a telephoto lens. The image was fuzzy, but she recognized a familiar face wearing an expression she hadn't seen in a long time.

"That's not Captain Rojo Herring," she said in a faint voice.

"Might I inquire as to how you are certain of this fact?"

"Because it's someone else."

"Who?"

"It's a long story," Dr. Presnelda told him. "And one that must absolutely be kept a secret. The shame on my family would be too great if the truth were known."

"Ma'am, you have my word."

And so Dr. Presnelda told him of her family's terrible, horrible secret. It was a scandal so scandalous that her face burned red with shame as she spoke. Detective Burton Sly thought he'd seen and heard it all, but her story was enough to make even his mouth hang open with wonder.

Last-Minute Preparations

When Jane got home from school that day, she learned that she and her brother and sister had been summoned to City Hall by their grandmother.

"I wonder what she wants," Penelope Hope said as the three of them walked over together.

"Who knows," Anderson Brigby Bright said. The summons had interrupted his plans to pick up the tuxedo he was going to wear to the Science Fair Dance from Fairwick's Formals. It was the finest tuxedo store in Remarkable—and therefore, the finest tuxedo store in the world.

But when they got to the mayor's office, they

discovered that Grandmama was not there. Instead, they were greeted by Stilton.

"Your grandmother has signed an official proclamation excusing you from school tomorrow," Stilton told them with a strained smile. The smile was strained because Stilton didn't like smiling any more than he liked talking to children. "You are to attend the bell-tower ribbon-cutting ceremony as her special guests."

"Do we have to?" Penelope Hope asked. She hated to miss school. She'd just started studying topographical algebra, which was much more interesting than a bell-tower ceremony.

"She told me to tell you that your presence is required."

"But that's not fair," Jane said. "If I don't go to school tomorrow, Captain Schnabel won't have anyone to teach."

"And I was planning on practicing my singing all day. The Science Fair Dance is tomorrow night!"

The smile on Stilton's face became even more strained as he looked at Anderson Brigby Bright.

"Your grandmother specifically requested that you not sing at all tomorrow. In fact, she indicated to me that this was the most important aspect of this proc-lamation."

"Why?" Anderson Brigby Bright was indignant.

"She mentioned something about not subjecting the crowds to . . ."

"Not subjecting them to what? My voice is getting quite good now."

"Ahhh, I think she mentioned something about being concerned about your singing destroying the goodwill of . . ."

"The people who've come to hear the bell tower would probably love to hear me. I'll prove it now by singing a bit of 'You Enchant Me, Yes You Do.' It's the song I'm going to serenade Lucinda with."

He cleared his throat. *"YEWWW ENCHAH-HHNT MEEEE, OW YESSSS YEWWWWW DOOOOO-ERGH."* It was a horrible noise—the worst that had ever come out of his throat, which was saying something.

"Anderson Brigby Bright, stop it!" Penelope Hope shouted. "Stop it right now!"

"Or at least don't do it while we're in the same room as you," Jane begged. "It's too much."

"What's the matter with everyone!" Anderson

Brigby Bright was getting angry now. "I'm good at this! Really good. I'm really good at everything." He stomped both feet this time.

"Of course you are," Stilton lied soothingly. "But I think . . . um . . . yes, I think your grandmother did mention something about the importance of resting your voice. You don't want to strain your vocal cords before your big performance."

Anderson Brigby Bright nodded slowly. "I hadn't thought of that. It's a good point. A very good point. I would hate not to sound my best for Lucinda."

"Wonderful," Stilton said. "I'll tell the mayor to expect the three of you tomorrow."

Then he ushered them out of the office quickly before any of them could change their minds.

Grandmama Julietta Augustina was not unsympathetic to Anderson Brigby Bright's attempts to win Lucinda's heart. She knew what it was like to fall head over heels in love with someone. Her grandson was so smitten that he reminded her of herself when she first laid eyes on Grandpa John.

But despite her appreciation for Anderson Brigby Bright's delicate emotional state, in this instance, her duty as mayor came first. Remarkable must continue to be the remarkable place it had always been. This meant making sure that the bell-tower ceremony was the kind of event that people would look back on fondly for the rest of their lives—something that would not happen if anyone heard Anderson Brigby Bright's singing. Keeping him quiet was the last thing she had left on her to-do list.

Which is why she was so puzzled to discover that she couldn't fall asleep that night.

"Hmph!" she told herself. Grandmama did not approve of not sleeping. It was a sure sign that she'd forgotten to take care of one of her important responsibilities that day—and like her daughter-in-law, she disapproved of forgetting responsibilities even more than she disapproved of sleeplessness.

She sat up to think through everything that needed to happen tomorrow. The bell tower had already been festooned with banners, bows, and balloons. The oversized, sapphire-encrusted scissors she would use for the ribbon cutting had been pulled out of storage and polished until they sparkled. Every available folding chair had been set up in the park next to the post office for the large crowds that were expected to gather, and the Remarkable Symphony Orchestra was ready to play a rousing composition written by Ludwig von Savage in honor of the event. She was certain that Ludwig was secretly hoping that everyone would think his composition was much lovelier than the music Ysquibel had written for the bell tower, but she was also certain that Ludwig was going to end up deeply disappointed.

She still needed to convince Dr. Pike not to leave town, but that could be dealt with once the bell-tower ceremony was over. But there was something else, something she wasn't thinking of.

Dr. Pike . . . Dr. Pike . . .

What had she been doing again when Mayor Chu called about Dr. Pike? She'd been talking to Grandpa John about . . . about . . .

Grandpa John had wanted to tell her something important. Something about the bell tower. She looked over at where her husband was lying next to her on the bed. He looked as ordinary sleeping as he did when he was awake, which made him all the more wonderful to Grandmama Julietta Augustina. She was wise enough to know that, despite what most people think, the best things in life are often quite ordinary.

"John!" she whispered. "John! Are you awake?"

He didn't stir, but Salzburg, who was perched on the bedpost on Grandmama's side of the bed, muttered "hmph" in her sleep.

"John?" Grandmama said one more time before giving up. She'd noticed that he'd been looking tired and worried lately. He probably needed his rest. In the morning, she would ask him what it was he had wanted to tell her.

The Opening Ceremony

The weather could not have been nicer for the bell-tower ceremony. The sun was bright without making the day hot, and there was a light breeze that was just cool enough to be refreshing without making anyone reach for a sweater. Crowds and crowds of people, even more than had been anticipated, showed up for the event. They waved small celebratory flags and listened to the Remarkable Symphony Orchestra. Small children ran around with helium balloons on their wrists. Everyone was giddy with the thrill of being part of such an unrivaled historic event.

Jane's father, who was accustomed to Remarkable's festivities, was overwhelmed by how much bigger and more celebratory this one seemed. He was extraordinarily proud of his talented wife, and he wanted to be able to tell her how excited the crowd was about the bell tower she'd designed. He also knew that if he ever needed to write a scene of a truly joyful and triumphant celebration in one of his novels, all he'd need to do was describe the scene unfolding before him.

Captain Rojo Herring had been among the first to arrive at the post office that morning. He wanted to make sure he got a seat in the front row so he could have an unobstructed view of the tower when it first began to chime. But the young girl who took the seat next to him was sobbing like her world was about to end.

"There, there, me child, it can't be as bad as all that, now can it?" Captain Rojo Herring said. He didn't really care about comforting her; he just wanted her to quiet down.

"What would you know about it?" the girl said, sniffling vigorously into a soaked handkerchief. "I've failed in the most important task of my life. The premiere is today, and Ysquibel remains lost."

"Ysquibel? Who be that?"

"He's the composer who wrote the song for the bell

tower. He has never, ever missed one of his premieres before, but now he's going to because I couldn't find him." Lucinda Wilhelmina Hinojosa's chic little glasses were fogged with her own tears.

"Well, perhaps he didn't want to be found," Captain Rojo Herring said comfortingly. "Perhaps he's happy staying lost."

This only made Lucinda wail harder. Captain Rojo Herring realized he'd better try a new tactic if he wanted her to quit making such a dismal racket.

"Look, ye don't know for a fact he's not 'ere. Look at this crowd. Maybe he be in there somewhere."

"I'm sure I would have recognized him."

"Maybe he be in a disguise or something. Did ye ever think of that? Now why don't ye stop yer blubbering and go off and look for 'im?"

Lucinda quit sobbing. She took off her fogged-up glasses and looked at Captain Rojo Herring with grateful and highly farsighted eyes.

"Of course! It's obvious. Why didn't I think of that!" She polished her glasses frantically and then put them back on her well-shaped nose so that she could look for disguised composers.

Meanwhile, Grandmama Julietta Augustina stood

on the top of the post office steps. The crowd was gathered before her. The cheerleaders from the gifted school were performing backflips, pyramids, basket tosses, and cradle catches in rapid succession. Misty McNeil, who was famous as the world's most exceptional fire dancer, tossed her flaming baton high in the air, then did a handstand and caught it with her toes as it came down.

Grandmama wasn't paying attention to the cheerleading or the fire dancing, which was just as well, since she was unlikely to have been impressed with either activity. She was watching Lucinda as she wandered around looking for someone. Grandmama smiled to herself, incorrectly assuming that Lucinda was searching for her handsome grandson. Maybe the Science Fair Dance would be as magical as Anderson Brigby Bright was expecting it to be.

Grandmama wished she felt as hopeful about the bell-tower ceremony. Despite the lovely weather and the cheerful crowds, she still had a nagging feeling that she'd overlooked something. She hadn't been able to ask Grandpa John what he had wanted to tell her because she hadn't been able to find him. He'd left the house before she'd woken up that morning so he could take Salzburg back to Captain Rojo Herring. Grandmama had not wanted to oversee the bell-tower ceremony with the parrot on her shoulder.

Then, just as the Remarkable Symphony Orchestra was winding down, she spotted Grandpa John standing at the edge of the crowd with Jane.

"Stilton," she said. "I need you to go fetch my husband."

"Who?"

"That man over there, who is next to that young girl. I have to ask him something."

Stilton reluctantly shook his head. "Madam Mayor, we're already behind schedule. You need to start the ceremony now."

He was correct. Time waits for no one, not even for a mayor as remarkable as Mayor Doe. The hands of the big clock on the new bell tower were pointing to 11:57.

"All right, Stilton. Get this crowd quieted down."

Stilton sent a signal to the cheerleaders to stop their acrobatics. He tapped on the microphone to get the attention of the crowd. And Grandmama Julietta Augustina stepped up to the podium.

"In three more minutes," she said, "the bells in

this tower will chime for the first time—and you will hear the finest bell-tower composition written by the finest living composer in the world." She stopped for a minute so that Ludwig von Savage could grumble to himself about being misunderstood and unappreciated. "And Remarkable, our fine, fine town, will become even more remarkable than before."

She looked over the crowd and gave Grandpa John a lovely smile. But Grandpa John didn't meet her eyes.

"Madam Mayor," Stilton hissed. The clock now read 11:58.

"I'd like to thank my daughter-in-law, Angelina Mona Linda Doe. Only an architect of such outstanding skill could have transformed our ordinary post office into the charming building you see before you. And I'd also like to thank Taftly Wocheywhoski, who not only completed the tower five months ahead of schedule, but was able to come in under budget as well."

Everyone applauded. Jane's mother and Taftly Wocheywhoski, who were standing next to Grandmama Julietta, bowed to the crowd. The clock hand moved to 11:59.

"And finally, I'd like to thank Ysquibel. I hope that wherever he is, he knows how much we appreciate having his delightful music grace our remarkable town. We are truly lucky."

Captain Rojo Herring gave a nervous cough. Grandmama glanced up and saw that the clock hand was moving toward 12 o'clock. Stilton handed her the large ceremonial scissors, and she snipped the ribbon in two. The crowd took a deep breath and held it, waiting for the first notes of the song to begin.

And they waited.

And they waited until it was hard to keep holding their collective breath.

But nothing happened.

Grandpa Gets Noticed

The silence that filled the air was more startling than any noise could have been. Grandmama looked at Stilton. Stilton looked at Angelina Mona Linda Doe. Angelina Mona Linda Doe looked at Taftly Wocheywhoski, and Taftly Wocheywhoski shrugged and ran up the bell-tower stairs to see what was wrong.

The crowd continued holding its breath, sure that any moment now the bells would begin to ring. Still nothing happened.

Finally, the crowd could wait no longer. The air was filled with a whooshing noise as everyone exhaled at the same time. Lucinda Wilhelmina Hinojosa let out a wail.

"Noooooooo!" she shrieked.

The clock hand moved to 12:01.

"Hmph!" Grandmama Julietta Augustina said. She was not accustomed to having things go wrong. She did not approve of it at all.

"This is terrible," Jane said to Grandpa John. "This is so truly bad."

Grandpa John did not reply. Just at that moment, Taftly Wocheywhoski stuck his head out of one of the bell-tower windows.

"It's the ropes!" he yelled. "The ropes that led from the bells to the mechanism that rings them. Someone's stolen every last one."

The crowd gasped.

"You!" Mrs. Peabody said as she angrily whacked Captain Rojo Herring with a metal gelato spade she happened to be carrying. "It was you, wasn't it? You've been obsessed with that bell tower since the first day you came here."

"Mrs. Peabody, yer making a dreadful mistake," Captain Rojo Herring said politely. "I be wanting to hear those bells chime as much as anyone. Why would I be taking the ropes?"

"Hmph," she said. "I don't trust you or your little

band of pirate friends any farther than I can throw you."

Captain Rojo Herring paled. "What do ye mean? I don't 'ave a band of pirate friends."

"Oh? Then I suppose I've been imagining those three smelly pirates who've been coming into my ice cream parlor asking for you."

"I . . . uh . . . oh dear," Captain Rojo Herring stammered as he looked around nervously. "Thar be three of them, you say?"

"I think someone should arrest that man," said Mr. Wembly. "He's certainly acting like a criminal."

"On the contrary," came a voice from the crowd. It was Detective Burton Sly. "Captain Rojo Herring is not the culprit. In fact, he's not even really a pirate."

Mrs. Peabody was outraged. "You're trying to tell me he's not a pirate? I suppose next you'll be telling me that the hat on his head which was blocking my view isn't a pirate hat, or that his three friends are shoe salesmen."

"Madam, I assure you that—"

"He's getting away!" screeched Mrs. Belphonia-Champlain. And sure enough, Captain Rojo Herring had hopped onto his bicycle and was pedaling away from the crowd just as fast as he could with peg legs.

"See? He's guilty!" Mrs. Peabody said triumphantly. "Look at him run."

"Madam," Detective Burton Sly said. "All he is guilty of is leaving before I had the chance to unmask the real culprit."

Detective Burton Sly strode through the crowd. Jane looked to see where he was headed, half expecting that he had the Grimlet twins in his sights. Who else would have come up with such a bold scheme?

But surprisingly, she didn't see the Grimlet twins anywhere. And more surprisingly, Detective Burton Sly seemed to be headed directly toward her.

"The culprit," Detective Burton Sly proclaimed, "is very average. Average height, average build, and has made the average number of mistakes in the commission of the crime. Additionally, this culprit has made one very amateur error—which is to say that the culprit has unwisely decided to return to the scene of the crime."

He stopped in front of Jane. Maybe he knew that Jane was a friend of the Grimlet twins. Maybe he even thought Jane was an accomplice! Or maybe the

Grimlet twins had framed her for a crime she hadn't committed. Jane was too nervous to say a word.

Then Detective Burton Sly did something unimaginable. Detective Burton Sly looked past Jane, lifted his hand, and pointed an accusing finger right at Grandpa John.

"You, sir, are the thief."

The crowd murmured angrily as everyone turned to stare at Grandpa John.

"I've never seen that man in my life!" Mrs. Peabody proclaimed huffily. She still thought someone should have stopped Captain Rojo Herring before he rode away.

"He's probably from the nearby town of Ding," said Taftly Wocheywhoski. "They have a shabby little bell tower they're extraordinarily proud of for some reason. I heard they were furious when they found out we were building a better one."

"Detective Burton Sly," Grandmama Julietta Augustina said coldly into the podium's microphone, "I'm afraid you've made a terrible mistake. There is absolutely no way that this man is guilty of anything."

"With all due respect, Madam Mayor, I wouldn't make a mistake in such a serious circumstance. But if you don't want to believe me, why don't you ask him for yourself."

"John," Grandmama said, "tell everyone here that you didn't steal those ropes."

But Grandpa John didn't answer her.

"John! Say you didn't steal them."

"I can't," Grandpa John said. "I did steal them."

"But why would you do such a thing?" Grandmama demanded. "You have to give them back right now."

"I can't," Grandpa John said again.

"Arrest him," Detective Burton Sly told two of his junior detectives. Jane watched in shock as her grandfather was handcuffed in front of her.

"No!" she cried. "Stop it!" She'd never felt so helpless in her life. Fortunately, right at that moment, Jane's dad arrived. He'd pushed his way through the crowd to defend his father.

"How dare you!" her dad bellowed at Detective Burton Sly. "As a prizewinning novelist, I order you to take those cuffs off immediately!"

"I'm afraid your literary prizes don't give you any jurisdiction in this particular instance, sir," Detective Burton Sly replied.

"You know nothing about jurisdictions—or literature!"

As the two men got into a heated argument about what kind of legal authority was bestowed by literary prizes, Grandpa leaned down to talk to Jane.

"Jane," he said in a voice too low for anyone but her to hear, "don't say a word about those ropes. Remember your promise."

"I can get them from Captain Schnabel," Jane whispered back. "Maybe they'll let you go if we return them."

Grandpa shook his head. "That bell tower must stay silent. In fact, just to be safe, go chop the ropes up into a million pieces and bury the pieces in a deep hole."

"But, Grandpa, why?"

"I don't have time to explain. But I'm counting on you."

Detective Burton Sly may not have been able to hear what Grandpa said, but he was a skilled enough detective to perceive the conspiratorial whispering that was occurring right behind him. He whirled around and scowled at Grandpa John. "What's that now?" he demanded. "What are you talking about?"

"I have nothing to say to you," Grandpa John told him.

"Don't you turn your back on me, Sly!!" Jane's father shouted indignantly as he jabbed the detective in the back. "We're not done with our argument yet!"

"Now just hold on a minute. Just let me ask this young girl what she and the suspect were whispering about. Young girl, I'd like to have a word with you, please."

But Detective Sly was too late. Jane was already gone.

"Did anyone see where that young girl went?" Detective Burton Sly called out. The people in the crowd murmured helplessly to each other. No one knew, because no one had been paying attention to Jane.

"Can anyone at least give me a description?" Detective Burton Sly asked. The crowd murmured helplessly again. No one had seen a thing.

A Captain Revealed

For the first time ever, Jane felt fortunate to be so undistinguished. No one had paid any attention to her at all as she slipped through the crowd. And now she was free to run to the public school as fast as her legs would carry her while her mind spun as fast as it could spin. Why on earth had her grandfather stolen the bell-tower ropes? She would never have believed he could do such a thing if she hadn't heard him confess. Still, he wanted her to trust him, and she did. If he said it was important for the ropes to be chopped into pieces and buried deep in a hole somewhere, she would do it.

Of course, there was the small matter of getting the ropes out of her classroom. This would be very difficult indeed if Captain Schnabel were there. She'd probably demand all kinds of explanations about why Jane wanted them, and Jane didn't have the foggiest idea what to tell her.

Jane glanced up at the sun—which counts as a lucky star in a pinch—and made a wish. "Please don't let Captain Schnabel be in there. Please let her have gone home as soon as she realized she wouldn't have any students in her classroom today."

Of course, Jane's wish would have been a lot more effective if it had also been a lot more specific. Instead of just wishing that Captain Schnabel were not at school, she should have wished that nobody was.

Jane flung open the door to the classroom—and then stopped dead in her tracks.

"Scuttle me eyes!" Jane exclaimed. She couldn't believe what she was seeing. Her classroom had been ransacked. The captain's wheel had been yanked out of the floor, the plank had been tossed out the window, and the Code of the Pirates had been ripped from the wall. Someone, possibly the Grimlet twins themselves, had been working hard to destroy every piece of pirate paraphernalia in the room. "Scuttle me eyes!" she repeated

"Watch your language, young lady!" came a voice. It belonged to the esteemed Dr. Presnelda—who was, for reasons that were unclear to Jane, angrily scrubbing the skull and crossbones off the blackboard.

"Where . . . where's Captain Schnabel?" Jane asked.

"*Ms.* Schnabel is at home," Dr. Presnelda snapped. "Thinking about what she's done. I've never seen a classroom in such a disgraceful state."

"I don't think it's a disgrace."

"I'm not the least bit interested in your opinion on this matter. You are not a highly regarded educator," Dr. Presnelda said, fixing Jane with an unfriendly stare. "And what are you doing here anyway? I thought you were excused from school today."

"Um . . ." Jane said, thinking furiously. "Um . . . I just stopped by to pick up a project I was working on so I could finish it over the weekend. I was keeping it over there." Jane pointed to the spot where Captain Schnabel had hung hooks to store the ropes. But now the hooks had been ripped out of the wall, and the ropes themselves were nowhere to be seen.

"Is this project related to piracy?" Dr. Presnelda asked.

"Uh-huh."

"Then most likely it's in the Dumpster out back."

"You threw my project in the Dumpster?" Jane said indignantly. It would be impossible for her to find the ropes in there. Every day, the school cafeteria workers made hundreds of hot meals just as if the public school were fully enrolled. Since Jane always brought a packed lunch from home and the Grimlet twins always stole each other's lunch money, every single meal was thrown away. By the end of the week, the Dumpster was a festering mess of rotting food and swarming flies.

"Of course I threw your project away. Piracy is not a proper subject for public school—and my sister, of all people, has no business teaching it. She made a promise to our family never to have anything to do with pirates."

"What's wrong with pirates?"

"Piracy reflects poorly on our family. Did you know we had to change our last name because of it?"

"No," Jane said, thinking that Dr. Presnelda wasn't making much sense.

"Presnelda isn't the last name I was born with— and my sister's real last name isn't Schnabel either. Before our family was disgraced, I was known as the esteemed Dr. Penzing."

"Penzing! You mean like Mad Captain Penzing the Horrific? Are you and *Ms.* Schnabel related to her?"

"Don't say that name!" Dr. Presnelda snapped. "And for the record, only I am related to Mad Captain Penzing the Horrific."

"But if you and Ms. Schnabel are sisters, then don't you both have to be related to Mad Captain Penzing?"

Dr. Presnelda sighed. "No wonder you never qualified for gifted education. Your reasoning skills are terrible. I'm related to Mad Captain Penzing *because* Ms. Schnabel is my sister."

Jane stared at her. "But . . . I don't understand. The only way that can be true is if Ms. Schnabel and Mad Captain Penzing the Horrific are the same person, and that doesn't make any sense at all."

"Doesn't it?" Dr. Presnelda smiled at Jane, but the smile was too full of contempt and impatience to be nice.

"I don't believe you!" Jane said stubbornly.

"No," Dr. Presnelda said. "You're not quite gifted enough to believe me, are you? Now shoo. I need to finish cleaning up this mess before anyone else finds out what my sister has done."

The Story of the Mad Captain

As soon as Jane left the public school, she put the whole idea that Ms. Schnabel was actually Mad Captain Penzing the Horrific out of her mind. She had more important things to worry about, such as the fact that Grandpa John had been hauled off to jail. And it was simply impossible for Jane to imagine that anyone like Mad Captain Penzing the Horrific would ever end up teaching in a fifth-grade classroom—especially in *her* fifth-grade classroom. Exciting things like that only happened to other people.

But Jane's failure of imagination did not change the fact that Dr. Presnelda happened to be telling the truth. And this truth would have been much easier to understand if Jane had only known more about Ms. Schnabel's early life.

Once upon a time, Ms. Schnabel was a young girl. No one called her Ms. Schnabel back then, of course. She was called by her given name, which was Mirabel Maisie, and she was well known in some circles for being a rather serious disappointment to her illustrious parents, Flip and Bitsy Penzing.

Flip and Bitsy loved good manners. Now, most people would agree that having good manners is important—but for some people, good manners are simply the most important thing in the world. These people, known as etiquette experts, believe that good manners are much more essential than fun, kindness, or love. As you might imagine, etiquette experts tend not to be particularly fun, kind, or loving—which is why they should never be parents. But the etiquette experts never understand this, and so they often have children anyway.

Flip and Bitsy Penzing were two of the most well-known etiquette experts in the world. They were so proper and dignified that they had not only written the book about how to live a gracious and decorous life, but had also hosted a television show and published a magazine on the topic as well. They knew the best way to host sumptuous dinner parties, grow exquisite herb gardens, and make even the dirtiest laundry smell like a field of daffodils. They had recipes for unforgettably delicious frosted cupcakes, and they knew how to construct dazzling homemade wreaths out of everyday objects.

Flip and Bitsy Penzing had many old-fashioned beliefs about parenting, which they felt would help Mirabel Maisie and their younger daughter, Ingrid Ann, grow up to be proper young ladies. They believed that children should be seen and not heard, so Mirabel Maisie and Ingrid Ann hardly said anything other than "please" and "thank you." They believed that children should be neat and tidy, so Mirabel Maisie and Ingrid Ann never played outside where there was dirt and never ate things like cookies or potato chips in case they got crumbs on their clothes. Flip and Bitsy also believed that children were happiest when busy doing chores, so Mirabel Maisie and Ingrid Ann spent most of their free time helping them cook their marvelous dinners, clean their gracious home, and construct their delightful craft projects.

Ingrid Ann had inherited her parents' love of

decorum and order, and so she thrived under her parents' care. But life was not so easy for Mirabel Maisie. Proper behavior did not come naturally to her. She developed nervous tics from having to sit still so often. Her face was pale and strained from lack of sunshine and fresh air. Loud inappropriate laughter sometimes escaped from her mouth for no particular reason. Worst of all, she began having recurrent nightmares about being chased by a spring salad made with arugula, pine nuts, and goat cheese, and being eaten alive by a properly worded thank-you note.

Her parents decided to send her off to summer camp in the hopes that it might revive her spirits—and because they still wanted her to act like a proper young lady, they shipped her off to a very respectable place known as Camp Doilyfeather. Instead of singing songs around a campfire or telling ghost stories, the young ladies at Camp Doilyfeather sat in a parlor each night and learned to make polite small talk and play the harp. Instead of making crafts out of leather and popsicle sticks, the young ladies at Camp Doilyfeather learned to embroider homilies on pillows and to decorate fancy hats for special occasions. And instead of learning how to hike, canoe, and ride horses, the young ladies at Camp Doilyfeather learned how to stroll with their parasols and practiced sitting with their legs crossed at the ankles.

It was during one of the long sessions of sitting with her legs crossed at her ankles that Mirabel Maisie had a sudden realization: She wasn't comfortable. In fact, sitting with her legs crossed at her ankles was extremely uncomfortable, and she couldn't understand why any young lady in her right mind would do it. And once she started thinking about it, she couldn't understand why anyone would want to do half the things her parents had taught her were important. It was all nonsense. Nonsense!

Mirabel Maisie uncrossed her ankles, and then recrossed her legs at the knees in an unladylike way and immediately felt much more comfortable.

"Miss Mirabel Maisie, what on earth do you think you're doing?" one of the Camp Doilyfeather counselors asked as she gave Mirabel Maisie a disapproving glare.

"Leaving," answered Mirabel Maisie rudely, and then she jumped out the parlor window and ran as fast as she could.

By the time Mirabel Maisie stopped running, she

found herself at a dockyard near the ocean. In front of her was a large ship called *The Wild Three O'Clock*, and hanging in one of its portholes was a "help wanted" sign.

Mirabel Maisie knew she couldn't go home. If she did, her parents would send her straight back to Camp Doilyfeather and make her write properly worded notes of apology for her unladylike behavior. So she walked up the gangplank and asked if she could have the job. She was asked to sign her name to a piece of paper for tax purposes, or so she was told, and hired on the spot.

But it was only after *The Wild Three O'Clock* had cast out to sea that Mirabel Maisie learned the truth. *The Wild Three O'Clock* wasn't just any ship. It was, in fact, a pirate ship commanded by Captain Two-Eyed Jake McSween, the fiercest and most feared pirate captain in all of the seven seas. And the piece of paper that Mirabel Maisie signed before she came on board was the Pirates' Code. By signing it, she promised to stay faithful to the ship and to attend to all of her pirate duties until their voyage was over.

Most young ladies who'd had such a proper upbringing might have been appalled to find themselves contractually obligated to serve on a pirate ship, but not Mirabel Maisie. For one thing, she found that swabbing decks, sharpening cutlasses, and stacking cannonballs wasn't nearly as much work as trying to maintain a proper and gracious home. Furthermore, she discovered that she loved life at sea. She liked being out in the sunshine and the salt air all day. She liked sleeping on the ship's deck and watching the stars at night. And she discovered she had a real aptitude for piracy. She was a natural at sword fighting, had an uncanny aim with a blunderbuss, and developed a real talent for drawing treasure maps.

Mirabel Maisie was also blessed with an unusual amount of pirate cunning, meaning that she knew how to scheme and manipulate the ship's politics to her favor. It didn't take her long to get promoted from deck-scrubber to dogsbody, then from dogsbody to boatswain, and then from boatswain to first mate. But Mirabel Maisie wasn't satisfied with being first mate. She stayed in the position just long enough to organize a mutiny, strand Captain Two-Eyed Jake McSween in the Bahamas, and take over as captain herself.

She soon became known in the pirating community as Mad Captain Penzing the Horrific. Captain Two-

Eyed Jake McSween may have been tough, but Mad Captain Penzing was ten times tougher, forty times meaner, and her exploits were a hundred times more legendary. All pirates knew that there was nothing more horrible than catching sight of *The Wild Three O'Clock* coming up fast on their starboard bow. She left no ship that crossed her path afloat, no battle unwon, and no treasure unplundered.

But even though she loved her new life at sea, she couldn't quite shake her upbringing. It didn't matter that her parents cared more about proper etiquette than they'd ever cared about her—they were still her parents, and she longed to make them proud.

So after she accidentally sunk *The Wild Three O'Clock* and was imprisoned in the port town of Ferragudo by the Portuguese Navy, she used her one phone call to contact them. She could have escaped without help, of course—breaking out of prison was easy for a pirate—but she wanted to use the opportunity to show her parents how well she had done for herself.

But her parents were not at all pleased with her success—and they told her in no uncertain terms that she had not only disgraced the family name, but that she was an embarrassment compared to her sister, Ingrid Ann, who'd gone to college to become an educator. The only way they could ever forgive her was if she promised to never, ever involve herself in piracy again.

And this is where Mirabel Maisie made a terrible mistake. She made that promise, trading the life she loved for one she hated and hiding her true self so well that even she had almost forgotten who she was. And now, even after years of unhappiness, she couldn't see a way to reverse that mistake without breaking her word.

At the Jail

The jail in Remarkable was another one of Jane's mother's great architectural masterpieces, even though it was one she rarely bragged about. Angelina Mona Linda Doe had crafted it to be so bleak and sad inside that the criminals incarcerated in it would be forced to rethink their criminal ways. All of the cells had hard cement floors, the walls were a particularly blah shade of gray, and there was nowhere to sit but on uncomfortable wooden benches.

Of course, when Angelina Mona Linda Doe was designing the jail, she probably never imagined that her own father-in-law would someday wind up in it, just as Jane had never imagined that she'd ever visit a prisoner there.

"I'd like to see John Doe, please," Jane told the junior detective who was sitting at the front desk in the jail's lobby.

"Who?" the junior detective asked.

"My grandfather. He was arrested this morning. He's . . . he's the man who stole the bell-tower ropes."

"Sorry," he said. "Can't help you."

"Why not?"

"It's against the rules."

"What rules?"

"The rules that say you need to be a grown-up to visit the prisoners."

"But that doesn't seem fair," Jane protested.

"What's not fair is him stealing those ropes," the junior detective told her. "He left a lot of people disappointed this morning. But don't worry. We'll set him free as soon as he tells us where he hid them."

"Oh," Jane said, her heart sinking like ropes in a Dumpster full of spoiled school lunches. "But what if I . . . er . . . he doesn't have them anymore?"

"Then I guess you can visit him when you grow up."

Jane went back outside. There was, as far as she could

tell, no rule about sitting on the jailhouse steps, so she found a spot shaded by an ornamental forsythia bush and tried to think of what to do next. But she hadn't been there for more than a minute when a straw wrapper few out of nowhere and hit her squarely in the chin.

"Ow!" Jane said indignantly, even though it didn't really hurt. She looked up to see that the Grimlet twins were standing on the sidewalk before her. They were struggling to carry a large wooden box with the words SCIENCE FAIR PROJECT stenciled on the side. The box was clearly very heavy, and the Grimlet twins seemed happy enough to set it down.

"So," Melissa said admiringly. "We hear your grandfather is a felon now. We'd be lying if we said we weren't envious."

"He's not a felon!"

"Really?" Eddie asked. "Because we heard he sabotaged the bell tower. It's absolutely brilliant—even if it is a bit pointless."

"Why is it pointless?"

"Because the town will just order new ropes and the bell tower will ring anyway."

"Unless we steal the new ropes," Melissa suggested excitedly.

"And then frame Jane's grandfather so that no one knows it's us."

"Excellent plan. And while we're at it we could—"

"Stop it!" Jane yelled. "You're not framing my grandfather. And you couldn't frame him even if you wanted to. They're not going to let him out of jail unless he gives the ropes back, and he can't do that, because I . . . well I . . ." Jane closed her mouth, sure she shouldn't say another thing.

"Jane?" Melissa asked. "Do you know something about the ropes you're not telling us?"

"No!" Jane said, but she was not a very good liar. Melissa looked at Eddie in delight.

"And here I thought she was much too boring to ever become a criminal."

"It's always the quiet ones that surprise us the most, isn't it?" Eddie said wisely.

"Stop it!" Jane said. "I don't want to talk about the ropes anymore. All I want to do is figure out how to get Grandpa John out of jail without them, okay?"

"You mean a jailbreak?" Eddie asked.

"A jailbreak could be fun," Melissa said. "Let's schedule it for the first thing on Monday."

"Monday? But that's three days from now!"

"We have a rather full weekend planned," Melissa explained.

"We'd hate to overextend ourselves," Eddie added. "Anyway, it's not like you can do it without us. You don't have a clue how to break someone out of a jail cell, do you?"

"Not exactly, but—"

"Monday will be here soon enough," Melissa said. "And you know what will help you pass the time? You could assist us in carrying this weather machine up to the top of Mount Magnificent. We need to get it to the gifted school."

"No," Jane said angrily. "If you won't help me get Grandpa out of jail right now, then I won't help you either."

"Suit yourself," Melissa said, not unkindly. "But on the bright side, jail might be the safest place for anyone to be tonight."

"It's true. Your grandfather might be the luckiest man in town."

"What's that supposed to mean?"

The Grimlet twins just smiled their wicked smiles, picked up their crate, and continued on their way.

"You're not the only criminals in Remarkable, you

know!" Jane bellowed after them. "Maybe I'll just ask someone else."

The Grimlet twins didn't even bother to turn around. They didn't think Jane really meant it. But they were quite wrong.

Jane had a plan. And in that moment, she was absolutely convinced of its brilliance.

The Pirates Versus the Grimlet Twins

If Jane had been paying closer attention in her conversation with the Grimlet twins, she might have noticed that they'd said something strange. They told her they wanted her help carrying their science fair project up Mount Magnificent. But the science fair was not being held at the gifted school. Instead, it was being held in the Great Exhibition Hall near the edge of town. The only event that was happening on Mount Magnificent that night was the Science Fair Dance.

"Ugh," Eddie said as he dropped his end of the weather machine crate with a heavy thud. "When we were designing this, why didn't we think to put wheels on it?"

"I thought of it," Melissa said as she dropped her end of the crate and shook out her arms. "I wrote it down in our plans. Then you stupidly forgot to install them."

"You're the one who's stupid. You never wrote down anything about wheels!"

"Don't get mad at me if you don't know how to read a simple schematic drawing in invisible ink," Melissa said smugly.

"Then don't be mad at me if I call you a lying scupperlout, you lying scupperlout."

"If I'm a lying scupperlout, then you're a whining renegado."

"If I'm a whining renegado, then you're a lily-livered labberneck," Eddie shouted, giving Melissa a shove.

"Did you just call me a labberneck?" Melissa asked as she shoved him back.

"I did, you labberneck."

As they hurled insults back and forth at each other, the Grimlet twins failed to notice that they were using the most colorful and elaborate examples of pirate-speak that Ms. Schnabel had taught them. They would have been horrified if they had realized it, since they tried never to learn anything at school.

But Jeb, Ebb, and Flotsam, who happened to be nearby, heard their shouting and recognized what they were doing immediately.

"There be only one place two landlocked rogue-lings could learn to shout at each other like that," Flotsam said to Jeb and Ebb.

"Aye," said Ebb. "They must 'ave come from that school with the pirate lessons."

"Which means they probably know the location of Captain Rojo Herring," Flotsam said. "So if we ask 'em all nice like, maybe they'll tell us where he be."

Of course, most pirates really don't know how to ask nicely, and asking the Grimlet twins about anything at that moment was a special challenge since their argument had moved past the insulting stage, through the shoving stage, and was now deep into the kicking-biting-and-throttling stage.

"Ahoy!" Flotsam yelled to get the Grimlet twins' attention. The Grimlet twins ignored him. The kicking-biting-and-throttling stage took a great deal of concentration.

"Ahoy!"

Flotsam gestured to Ebb and Jeb, and they each

grabbed a twin by the scruff of the neck and pulled them apart.

"Now what's all this about then?" Flotsam said. "Can't you two snips stop yer fighting long enough to have a civilized conversation with the likes of us?"

"Why should we want to talk to you?" Melissa said, twisting around to kick Jeb in the shin.

"We just have one little question for you, then we'll let you get back to yer brawling, savvy? Now who taught the two of you all of those lovely pirating phrases you've been hurling at each other?"

"That's none of your business," Eddie told him as he struggled to break free of Ebb's grip.

"In fact it's top secret," Melissa said.

"Highly confidential," Eddie added. "Classified, even."

"Really?" Flotsam asked.

"No. Not really," Eddie said. "We just don't want to tell you anything."

Flotsam scowled. "I see," he said. "So you wouldn't want to tell me if that book I see lying on the ground over there belongs to you?"

Melissa and Eddie looked. The Book of Dangerous Deeds and Dastardly Intentions had fallen out of

Melissa's backpack during their scuffle and was now lying in the dirt. Eddie opened his mouth and closed it again. Melissa managed to defiantly mumble, "Never seen it before."

"Then you won't be minding if I be ripping some of the pages out then, would ye now?"

Eddie paled and Melissa turned green, but neither of them spoke.

"Or perhaps," Flotsam said, pulling a match out of his pocket and lighting it on the heel of his pirate boot, "I'll just burn it up while you watch. How does that sound to ye?"

The Grimlet twins tried to act tough. They tried not to mind that years worth of wicked schemes and horrible plots were about to be reduced to ash. But as Flotsam's match singed the first page of their beloved book, it became too much to bear.

"We'll talk! We'll talk!" Melissa shrieked.

"Anything you want to ask us!" Eddie promised desperately. "Just give it back."

Flotsam blew out the match as Ebb and Jeb released their grips on the Grimlet twins.

"That be more like it. I knew you could be reasonable-like," Flotsam said. "Now, we be missing a captain, see? And we have it on good authority that 'e ran away to this 'ere town to start a new life as a schoolteacher."

"And why do you think we'd know anything about that?" Eddie asked.

"Because someone's been teaching you two to cuss like pirates, and we're thinking that person be our missing captain. So tell us where this teacher of yers be."

"And then you'll give us our book back?" Melissa asked.

"Pirate's honor," Flotsam told her.

Melissa and Eddie conferred for a moment. Then Eddie nodded and turned back to the pirates.

"We'd be more than delighted to help you in exchange for our book. Our teacher likes to go by the name of Captain Schnabel and does seem to have a rather thorough understanding of piracy. Much more than you might expect from a regular schoolteacher."

"And where can we find this Captain Schnabel?"

"That's easy," Melissa said. "She lives in a tidy yellow house with flowers in the front. It's about two blocks east of the library."

"Now that wasn't so hard, was it?" Flotsam said, handing Melissa back the book. But Ebb was not so easily appeased.

252

"Now 'ang on a minute there. Did you say *she* lives two blocks from the library?"

"I did," Melissa said. "Yellow house. Flowers. You can't miss it."

"But our captain ain't a she. Our captain is a he."

"Arghh!" Flotsam yelled. "That no-good detective has given us another worthless lead. A pox on 'im!"

"A pox on 'im," Jeb seconded enthusiastically, then he stopped and thought for a moment. Thinking and standing at the same time was almost more than Jeb was capable of, so he held on to Ebb's arm to keep from falling over. "Unless, of course, Captain Rojo Herring be disguising himself as a woman."

"Aye. It could be," Ebb said, looking at Melissa and Eddie. "Be it possible that yer Captain Schnabel be our Captain Rojo Herring dressed up as a woman?"

The Grimlet twins shook their heads.

"No. Not possible."

"In fact, it's completely impossible."

"And why be it so impossible?" Jeb snarled. He had good ideas so rarely that he hated to see one dismissed without much discussion.

"Because Captain Rojo Herring is an entirely different person who lives in an entirely different house that's nowhere near the library," Eddie told him.

"You know wheres Captain Rojo Herring be?"

"Of course we do," Melissa said. "And you could have saved us all a lot of hassle if you'd just told us that's who you were looking for in the first place."

"Well, tell us where he be! Tell us now!" Ebb said. He could hardly believe that they were so close to finding their missing captain.

"Um . . . no," Melissa said.

"Why not?"

"Because we don't have to, you see," Eddie explained. Melissa had put The Book of Dastardly Deeds and Dangerous Intentions back in her backpack where Flotsam couldn't get to it again. "Of course, we might be persuaded to help you, if you did something for us first."

"What do you want from us?" Ebb asked warily.

"Just a small task," Eddie said. "We have something rather heavy we need carried to the top of Mount Magnificent. If you help us with that, then we'll happily tell you where to find Captain Rojo Herring."

To the Mansion

Jane could not quit smiling to herself as she hurried up the trail toward the Mansion at the Top of Remarkable Hill and contemplated her brilliant plan. The Grimlet twins would be so surprised come Monday when they learned that she'd managed to rescue her grandfather without them. Captain Rojo Herring was a better choice to help her than they had been. As an experienced pirate, breaking someone out of jail was probably as easy for him as tying his own shoes—or at least it would be if he had feet instead of peg legs.

Unfortunately, Jane's plan was not nearly as brilliant as she thought it was. A truly brilliant plan would have recognized that Dr. Presnelda's revelations about Ms. Schnabel went a long way toward explaining her teacher's behavior in the last few weeks. And if Jane had understood Mad Captain Penzing the Horrific and Ms. Schnabel were the same person, she might have made the wise decision of going to her for help instead. But, predictably, Jane's plan was average instead of brilliant, and so she turned to a person who couldn't even help himself.

As Jane ran to the Mansion at the Top of Remarkable Hill, a sudden, chilly gale rushed up the mountainside. Jane looked at the sky and saw that the west wind was pushing dark anvil-shaped clouds toward the town.

"That's strange," Jane said. The clouds looked like cumulonimbus storm clouds—a fact Jane knew from doing the same weather work sheet over and over again. But according to the weather forecast that morning, the weather in Remarkable was supposed to be even more pleasant than usual.

Then Jane heard a wild screech and saw a small, feathered figure flapping vainly against the wind. It was Salzburg, trying to stay aloft in the rough weather. But the wind was too much for the parrot, and she lost control. She cartwheeled through the air and hit the ground with a loud thump.

"Salzburg!" Jane cried as she rushed over to the bird. "Are you okay?"

The parrot had lost a few feathers and seemed a little dazed, but other than that, she was unharmed.

"Come on, I'll take you home."

Salzburg growled at this suggestion—she would much rather Jane took her back to Grandmama at City Hall—but when the wind blew again and brought a faint murmur of thunder with it, she settled onto Jane's shoulder without so much as another grumble.

The cumulonimbus storm clouds were nearly overhead by the time Jane finally reached the Mansion at the Top of Remarkable Hill. She rang the doorbell and almost immediately heard Captain Rojo Herring's voice from inside.

"I'm coming! I'm coming!" he yelled. "But you can start unloading it onto the driveway if you want. I don't have much time." He had a big, expectant smile on his face as he opened the door—a smile that slid away as soon as he saw Jane.

"Oh," he said dismally. "It's only you."

"Sorry," Jane said, wishing she were someone he'd be gladder to see.

"I thought you were the Munch jelly delivery

person. I just placed an expedited emergency jelly order. Now, I don't mean to be rude, but I'm in a dreadful hurry and I don't have time to talk." He started to close the door in Jane's face.

"Wait!" Jane said. "I have your parrot."

"Oh. Good," he said, sounding insincere. "I was afraid I might have to leave her behind."

"Behind what?" Jane asked. Captain Rojo Herring was acting quite strange—and he was suddenly speaking much more like a normal person and less like a pirate.

"Uh . . . it's not important," he said. He checked his watch and then peered down the driveway. "I do wish my jelly order would hurry up and arrive."

"Well, um, while you're waiting, I was wondering if I might get your advice about something." Jane was nervous. "It's about my grandpa. You probably don't remember him."

"Of course I remember him. He's an extraordinary man. I met him out at Lake Remarkable one night."

Jane was sure that the captain had mixed her grandfather up with someone more interesting, but now was not the time to explain this. "He's been arrested," Jane told him.

"He has? What on earth for?"

"For stealing the ropes to the bell tower."

"Great heavens! So he's the saboteur, huh? I wonder if it has anything to do with Lucky."

"Why would it have anything to do with Lucky?"

"Well, she loves beautiful music even more than she loves those figgy doodles he feeds her. Maybe he was worried about the effect the bell-tower music would have on her. I know how much he wants to protect her."

"But Grandpa John doesn't know anything about Lucky," Jane said.

"Sure he does. Just ask him."

"I can't! At least not unless we break him out of jail. I'm going to need your help to free him."

"What?" Captain Rojo Herring said. "Why would you think I'd be able to help you?"

"Because you're a pirate—and Captain Schnabel said that pirates knew all about things like that. I mean surely you've had to escape from the brig before . . ." Her voice trailed off. For the first time she noticed that Captain Rojo Herring's house was in disarray. His clothes had been shoved into a duffel bag. About half of the books from his bookshelves were piled into moving boxes. Even his piano was wrapped up in a padded furniture blanket that was secured by ropes.

"Are you going somewhere?" Jane asked. Captain Rojo Herring sighed sadly and gestured for Jane to come inside.

"I have to get out of town as fast as I can. My old pirating crew has very nearly caught up with me."

"So I suppose this means you don't have time to help me," Jane said despondently.

Captain Rojo Herring shook his head. "I couldn't help you anyway, Jane. What that detective said today at the bell tower was right. I'm . . . I'm not a real pirate."

"What!" Jane said. "But what about the hat? What about your pegs legs! What about your pirate clothes?"

"Fakes. All fakes. The peg legs screw over my real ones. My outfit is just a costume I borrowed from . . . well, never mind where I got it."

"I don't understand," Jane said. "Why would you pretend to be a pirate?"

"It's hard to explain. I used to have a job, you see. It was a job I didn't like very much, and I wanted to get away from it."

"What kind of job?" Jane asked.

"It's not important. But I was good enough at it that no one wanted me to do anything else, even though I was sick of doing the same thing over and over."

"How did you get away?"

"One day, I found myself dressed as a pirate. It . . . well, it made sense if you were there. And I was a little bit hungry, so I went out and got myself something to eat. I guess no one recognized me, because for the first time in as long as I could remember, no one asked me about . . . about my work. It was the most relaxing meal I'd ever had. So I kept the pirate suit. And every so often I'd dress up in it and go out on my own. And then one day, I got carried away and joined a pirate ship as the captain."

"But you didn't like it?"

"No. I hated being at sea almost as much as I hated doing what I was doing before. The only difference is that I wasn't much good at sailing. So one day, I crashed my ship on a coral reef and put a hole in its bow. While my crew was fixing it, I slipped away and escaped. But now they've tracked me to Remarkable," he said with a sigh. Then he looked out the window toward the balcony where he'd seen his mystery woman. "I think I could have been very happy here."

"You could stay anyway," Jane said.

The doorbell rang. Captain Rojo Herring brightened again. "It's the delivery truck. Would you do me a favor and answer that? I don't think I can bear to start a new life without some of that fantastic Munch jelly to see me through."

"Sure," Jane said.

But it was not the driver of the jelly truck who had rung the doorbell. Indeed, the driver of the jelly truck had been forced to turn back when a sudden rainstorm had washed out the road between Munch and Remarkable.

So Jane was utterly and completely taken by surprise when she opened the door, because what she found on the other side were three mean and smelly pirates.

The Science Fair Dance

It would be nice to be able to say that Jane and Captain Rojo Herring put up a good fight against the combined forces of Jeb, Ebb, and Flotsam. It would have been nice to say that they at least held their ground for a short while. But alas, this would not be even slightly accurate.

Captain Rojo Herring was captured before he'd even had a chance to turn and run—and Jane soon found herself locked inside Salzburg's enormous parrot cage so she wouldn't bother anyone by going for help.

Jane did her best to escape. She kicked at the birdcage's door, shook the bars with her fists, and yelled and screamed for someone to let her out. It was to no avail. There was no one to hear her. She feared she'd be stuck in the cage until someone noticed that she was missing—and by then, it would be much, much too late to save Captain Rojo Herring.

When she had worn herself out, she leaned back against a wooden bird perch and tried to think what to do next. She'd heard once that people could focus their minds and send messages to loved ones when they were in trouble. She knew her brother would be at the school dance by now, and she knew that the Mansion at the Top of Remarkable Hill had a clear line of sight to the top of Mount Magnificent. She closed her eyes and did her best to send him an urgent mental message, hoping he would come to her rescue.

Unfortunately, this was even less effective than kicking and screaming had been. Anderson Brigby Bright wasn't thinking about Jane even a little bit. His entire focus was on Lucinda Wilhelmina Hinojosa.

After so many months of worry and anticipation, Anderson Brigby Bright could hardly believe he was actually at the Science Fair Dance with her. He wanted to draw a picture of the moment so that he could keep it forever, but he feared that it might appear he was

264

showing off if he got out his oil paints and asked her to hold her position for the next hour. And he didn't want anything to ruin his perfect evening.

Not that the evening had been perfectly perfect so far. Anderson Brigby Bright had already been forced to overlook a few small glitches—some of which might be considered his fault. For example, he'd been so excited for the evening to start that he'd arrived at Lucinda's house a few minutes early. He assumed that she, like he, would have spent most of the day getting ready. He was a little surprised when she answered the door in an old pair of sweatpants and an oversized red T-shirt that complemented the color of her eyes, which were bloodshot and swollen from weeping.

Then, oddly, she seemed to have no idea what he was talking about when he said he'd come to take her to the dance. She didn't even seem to want the wrist corsage he'd brought for her—not even after he pointed out how well its exotic flowers matched his small yet elegant boutonniere.

He might have still been on the porch trying to persuade her that it was time to leave if her mother hadn't intervened. She told Lucinda that she might as well go do something fun like go to a school dance instead of sulking about Ysquibel in her room. Lucinda had then screamed "You've never understood me or my torment!" before her mother replied "That's absolutely enough, Lucinda!" and shoved her daughter out the front door.

The only thing Lucinda wanted to talk about as they walked to Remarkable's School for the Remarkably Gifted was how her unreasonable mother didn't appreciate her musical passions. Anderson Brigby Bright tried to sympathize, but this was difficult because he'd never met anyone who didn't appreciate him.

And now, at last, they were together at the dance. Despite her informal attire, Lucinda looked beautiful under the twinkling lights that hung over the gifted school's outdoor courtyard. Giant woven tapestries of the periodic table hung down from the roof of the school's gymnasium, and twirling models of DNA double helices dangled from nearby trees. They were standing right next to an ice sculpture of the Large Hadron Collider, which was so detailed that it looked as if it might start circulating high-energy proton beams at any moment. It was all too romantic.

"Are you as happy as I am, Lucinda Wilhelmina Hinojosa?" Anderson Brigby Bright asked as he looked soulfully into her red-rimmed eyes. She just stared back at him—the kind of deep and meaningful stare that a girl gives a boy when she thinks he's being especially stupid.

"This is the worst day of my life," she told him.

"It is?" He couldn't imagine what she was talking about. He'd caught a glimpse of his reflection in the punch bowl and knew he looked debonair. Most of the other girls at the dance had swooned with jealousy when Lucinda walked in with him.

"I've had this day marked on my calendar for months. I've never been so disappointed."

"You're disappointed?" Anderson Brigby Bright was starting to get confused.

"Of course I'm disappointed! I was supposed to hear the latest and probably greatest composition by Ysquibel today. But it didn't happen. It's even more disappointing than not being able to locate him after months and months of trying."

"You're still thinking about Ysquibel?" he asked incredulously. She was clearly wasting her time obsessing about that musician when she could be enjoying his company. Despite the fact his own grandfather had been arrested, he hadn't given the bell tower a second thought since learning it had been sabotaged. But then, he wouldn't have given it a second thought even if it had worked perfectly.

"Now there is absolutely nothing to look forward to. Nothing!"

"Now now, that's not true, dear Lucinda," Anderson Brigby Bright said, hoping to cheer her up. "I've prepared the most marvelous surprise for you.

Lucinda Wilhelmina Hinojosa groaned. "It's not another painting, is it?"

"What if it was? You'd be lucky to get another painting. I'm going to be quite famous one day."

"You're going to be famous as a *painter*." She said the word "painter" like it was a particularly vile form of toe fungus. "That's not like really being famous. Not like being a musician."

"How dare you!" Anderson Brigby Bright shouted. He didn't mean to sound so angry, but he couldn't help himself.

"If a painter went missing, no one would even bother to form regional clubs to look for him. He could just stay missing forever and no one would even notice."

Anderson Brigby Bright opened his mouth and then closed it again. He didn't want to ruin his perfect evening by fighting with Lucinda, no matter how wrong and crazy she was being.

"As I mentioned before, I've prepared a surprise for you," Anderson Brigby Bright said. He made himself smile even though what he really wanted to do was clench his teeth. "It's not a painting and I think you'll quite like it."

He left the table and went up to the microphone. He signaled for the band to start playing the opening bars of "You Enchant Me, Yes You Do."

But just before he filled his lungs to belt out the first note, he had a moment of doubt. What if Jane was right? What if he really wasn't a gifted singer, despite all of his practicing?

No. He couldn't stop now. Lucinda Wilhelmina Hinojosa was watching him, and she deserved nothing less than greatness. He opened his mouth and prepared to sing.

But just as the first horrible note of the song came out of his throat, it was drowned out by a deafening clap of thunder. The band stopped playing as the lights in the trees flickered on and off. And then a storm like no other broke over the Science Fair Dance.

The Storm of the Century

Oh how it rained! The clouds boomed the loudest thunder in the history of thunder, and the sky was lit up by the flashiest lightning in the history of lightning flashes.

Students at the Science Fair Dance scattered in all directions. The crepe paper decorations dissolved into mushy puddles. The lights in the trees blew down in a tangle of sparking electric wires. The punch bowl overflowed with rainwater, and the dance floor grew squishy and slick.

Anderson Brigby Bright Doe III found himself separated from Lucinda Wilhelmina Hinojosa in the commotion. He'd taken shelter in the gazebo, and she had taken refuge in the bandstand.

Anderson Brigby Bright was scared of thunderstorms, although this was not something he would admit, even to himself. So when his hands began to shake and his knees began to tremble, he told himself that he was only concerned for Lucinda. He thought about bravely making his way across the courtyard to the bandstand to be with her. It seemed so romantic to hold each other's hands for comfort during the storm.

KABOOM!

As the whole courtyard shook from an exceptionally close lightning strike, Anderson Brigby Bright reminded himself of how she'd said that no one would care if a painter went missing. He could just barely make out the bandstand through the torrents of rain that were pouring down—torrents that would undoubtedly flatten his wonderfully wavy hair into a dripping mess—and decided to stay where he was. Maybe after she endured the storm with nothing but the comfort of a bunch of musicians and musical instruments she'd realize how crazy she'd been acting and learn to appreciate him and his photorealistic paintings more.

Across town, Ms. Schnabel was once again standing on her front porch in her fuzzy pink slippers. She was watching the rain pour down in front of her as the sky lit up with brilliant flashes of light.

She was not supposed to be at home. She was supposed to be up at the gifted school helping to chaperone the Science Fair Dance. Her sister had insisted that she volunteer as a way to demonstrate her commitment to her new life as a teacher instead of her old one as a pirate.

She took a deep breath, filling her lungs with the wildness of the night. Back when she was a pirate captain, she had adored nights like this. She'd climb up the mast to the crow's nest, letting the wind and rain lash at her while her crew huddled belowdecks. She always felt safe on *The Wild Three O'Clock*, no matter how the ship pitched in the waves. It was a worthy vessel, although in the end, she hadn't been a worthy captain. Her own pride had sunk her ship when no storm could. The wind howled around the front porch, almost as if it were as brokenhearted as she was that *The Wild Three O'Clock* now lay at the bottom of the Sea of Cortez.

BLAM! BOOM! BANG!

Three flashes of lightning were followed quickly by three crashes of thunder. The intensity of the storm had caught Ms. Schnabel by surprise. Normally she was very good at sensing what the weather would be like—and her senses had told her that the evening was going to be perfectly pleasant. It wasn't like her to be wrong about a weather prediction.

Of course, maybe she hadn't been wrong. Maybe something else had happened to disturb the pattern of the weather. Maybe the Grimlet twins had accomplished what they'd set out to accomplish.

"No," she told herself. "That's impossible!"

But was it? What if the Grimlet twins had succeeded? What if they really had built a weather machine that worked well enough to generate such a powerful storm?

The rain was blowing up onto the porch now, and her fuzzy pink slippers were starting to get drenched. She went back into the house and looked at the very proper and modest organza silk dress that her sister had set out for her to wear. But she couldn't put it on now. Her mother had taught her that organza silk was a poor choice for bad weather because it was easily stained by water spots.

Of course, with the storm, the Science Fair Dance was probably canceled anyway. There was no point heading there now.

Her eyes drifted over to the kitchen trash can. Her pirating clothes were inside of it. They were waterproof and couldn't get any more stained than they already were. They'd be perfect for a night like this. Surely she wouldn't be hurting anyone if she put them on one last time and went to see what the Grimlet twins were up to.

Unlike real pirating clothes, pirate costumery is not terribly waterproof. This was something that Captain Rojo Herring was learning the hard way as he was dragged down to the lake by his three captors. His clothes were sodden, his peg legs were waterlogged, and his magnificent pirate hat was wetter than a wet blanket.

He wanted very much to wipe the small river of water that was running down his face and dripping down the front of his shirt, but he couldn't, because Ebb had tied his hands together—and he would have liked to complain about having his hands tied together, but Jeb had put a gag in his mouth to keep him from yelling for help. Not that it mattered. No one could have heard his cries over the noise of the storm.

He'd always told himself that there was no fate on earth worse than being the fake captain of a real pirate crew. Now he realized he was wrong. Being the real prisoner of a real pirate crew was much, much worse. As Captain Rojo Herring was forced on board *The Mozart Kugeln*, he worked frantically to untie the knots that bound his wrists. His long fingers were strong and nimble, but he was running out of time.

"Unfurl the sails," Flotsam told Jeb, raising his voice so that he could be heard over the growling thunder. "We'll soon be underway."

"As long as the wind don't rip us to pieces," Ebb grumbled. "I don't like this storm. It ain't natural."

"It's because we're cursed, ain't it," Jeb said. "That pizza psychic woman be right. Nights like this be when the Mad Captain goes hunting fer treasure."

"Stop saying that name!" Flotsam snapped. "You want to bring *The Wild Three O'Clock* down on us all?"

The Mozart Kugeln twisted and tossed in the storm. The three pirates grimly fought to keep the ship under control.

"Maybe she'll leave us alone," Ebb pointed out. "All we got on board is our prisoner, and 'e ain't worth much."

"Not unless Mad Captain Penzing thinks music be treasure," Jeb said. "You'll play for us again, once we get back to the ship, won't ye? We missed the sound of yer fiddle lulling us off to winky winks at night."

Captain Rojo Herring made muffled noises through his gag. But whether he was agreeing or disagreeing with the request was impossible to say.

A sudden burst of lightning lit up the lake so that it was almost as bright as day—and Ebb, who was serving as the lookout, saw something lean and large gliding through the water.

"Did you see that?" he gasped.

"What?"

"That thing. Moving in the water. It's big."

"Yer imagination's getting the better of ye, you chowderhead."

Captain Rojo Herring began mumbling frantically through his gag. He'd seen the shape, too—and he'd seen that it had changed its course and was now moving toward *The Mozart Kugeln*.

"It ain't me imagination," Ebb said. "It's . . . it's . . ."

"Is it Mad Captain Penzing the Horrific?" Jeb asked innocently.

"A plague on yer scurvy head!" Flotsam shrieked at him. "Don't say that name!"

But it was too late. The large shape suddenly loomed

up in front of them. The three pirates screamed—and Captain Rojo Herring would have screamed, too, if he'd been able to with a gag in his mouth. Then the shape smashed into the bow, and the boat capsized.

As Captain Rojo Herring sank to the bottom of Lake Remarkable, he realized he'd made a tactical error. It was all well and good he'd learned to ride a bicycle, but in retrospect, he wished he'd learned to swim first. Riding a bicycle is not such a useful skill when one finds oneself suddenly thrown from a boat in the middle of a large body of water.

He'd managed to finish untying his wrists, but having his arms free did not help him much. He flailed frantically, but everything he did seemed to make him sink even faster. And as he sank, he realized just how much he had to lose. He wanted to stay in Remarkable and enjoy life in his new house. He wanted to find the woman he loved and convince her that she loved him, too. Most of all, he wanted to not spend the rest of his life running from people who wanted him to be something he wasn't.

But now it was too late. His lungs were bursting in his chest, desperate for air. His head was growing bleary and his arms were growing weak. Then, just when he thought things couldn't get much worse, they suddenly did.

The large object, the one that had capsized the boat, was rapidly swimming toward him. It had dark turquoise skin, large horns, and a mouth full of the sharpest teeth he could ever remember seeing.

It was Lucky, of course, even if it was hard to recognize her as the same creature who had happily danced to his music that night at the lake. She did not look the least bit happy now. The earsplitting cracks of thunder had driven her out of her mind with terror and anxiety. Her serpentine tail thrashed as she rapidly propelled herself toward Captain Rojo Herring. He saw anger in her wild eyes, as if she were blaming him for the storm.

Lucky snapped at his head and missed. Captain Rojo Herring paddled away from her as best he could. The lake monster let out a wild, underwater roar and raised her head to snap at him again. Captain Rojo Herring closed his eyes, knowing he could not escape being crushed between her strong, sharp teeth.

Jane Makes a Discovery

It was true what they said about the Mansion at the Top of Remarkable Hill. It was drafty. Jane shivered in her birdcage as wind whipped around the mansion and seeped in through the cracks and under the doors. Rain lashed the roof, and the mansion creaked with awful groans and wild rattles. At least Jane hoped the groans and rattles were coming from the mansion and not from the ghosts that were supposed to haunt it. If only she'd read about the mansion's ghosts when Ms. VanderTweed had offered her the book about them!

A sudden gust of wind battered the roof, and the mansion shook as if it were an effort to stay up under the assault of the weather. Salzburg frantically flapped

279

around the living room and knocked over a Boston fern that had been sitting atop a sturdy bookcase.

"Salzburg, don't be scared," Jane said soothingly. "Come down here instead and show me how you get out of your cage."

Salzburg screeched and called Jane a scurvy dog. The storm had unnerved the bird quite badly, and all she wanted to do was hide her head beneath her wing.

Jane wished she had a wing so she could stick her head under it, too. Being stuck in a birdcage was a tiresome end to a long and unsettling day. First Grandpa had gotten arrested, then Dr. Presnelda had tried to convince her that Captain Schnabel was actually a pirate, and Captain Rojo Herring had told her he definitely wasn't one. And stranger still was the ridiculous thing Captain Rojo Herring had said about Grandpa John knowing Lucky. People like her grandfather didn't make friends with lake monsters. And they didn't commit crimes to protect them, did they?

But what if Captain Rojo Herring was right? What if Grandpa John really had sabotaged the bell tower to protect Lucky? What if he really did go to the lake to feed her figgy doodles? It would be amazing. Totally amazing, but . . .

Jane tried to ignore the pang of jealousy burning in her stomach. If Grandpa were as impressive as everyone else in Remarkable, it would mean that she was truly the only one in town who wasn't special at all.

So now, in addition to feeling cold, frustrated, and scared, Jane also began to feel more alone than she ever had in her life. It was hard not to cry. In fact, it was impossible not to cry—and tears started streaming down her face. She looked around for something she could use to wipe them away, but all she could find were the newspapers that lined the bottom of the birdcage. Newspapers are not particularly absorbent, and Jane knew they were likely to turn into a soggy, inky mess if she got them wet, but she sensibly realized that having something to read might go a long way toward taking her mind off her troubles.

Jane had hoped she'd find the comics, or a weather report, or maybe even the section of classified ads where people listed puppies for sale. But as she dried her eyes on the corner of her shirtsleeve, she discovered something rather odd. Captain Rojo Herring hadn't lined the birdcage with full newspaper sections. Instead, he'd used a mishmash of newspaper clipping and stories he'd cut out of magazines. It was almost as if he'd been collecting them to save, but then had changed his mind.

Odder still was the fact that every single article Captain Rojo Herring had collected was about Ysquibel. Why would a pirate—even a fake pirate—be so interested in a musician?

"It's because they're friends, isn't it?" Jane said to herself, remembering how Ysquibel had named a character Captain Rojo Herring in his musical *Prise de Corsaire*.

Jane began to read. As the night wore on, she learned all about how Ysquibel had developed a gift for music at an early age—and that his gift meant he spent his childhood composing and performing with no time to go to school, play with friends, or do anything else. As he'd grown older, his schedule had only become more intense.

His fans were as demanding as they were adoring. When he asked for a night off, they protested vigorously. When he wanted to go on vacation, there were riots in the streets. He tried to explain that he was utterly and completely sick of creating music, but no one cared. He talked endlessly about all the things he'd like to do with his life instead of being a famous composer, but no one paid any attention to this—until the night he disappeared.

"So he was stuck in a job he hated, too," Jane mused. The musician and the pirate captain seemed to have more in common than just a friendship.

There had been several sightings of Ysquibel since he'd gone missing. The most recent one was on Kaffeklubben Island north of Greenland. Kaffeklubben Island was so far-flung that it was only accessible by boat. Jane wondered if maybe Captain Rojo Herring had taken Ysquibel there before he wrecked his pirate ship. It was what a good friend would do.

And then, without warning, the bottom of the birdcage broke. Jane fell out and landed hard on the floor below. She was quite surprised by this, but she shouldn't have been. Birds, even large ones like the great bustard of Central Europe, are not heavy. Consequently, birdcages aren't designed to support the weight of an average ten-year-old, not even one as average as Jane.

Jane scrambled to her feet. She was bruised from the fall, but happy to be out of the cage. Maybe, just maybe, there was still time to save the captain. And once she'd saved Captain Rojo Herring, then he could help her save Grandpa John! Getting help from a fake pirate would be better than nothing.

She ran to the telephone to call for help, but the line was dead because of the storm. Then she ran to the front door and tried to open it, but the pirates had locked it and taken the key. She kicked and pounded on it while Salzburg flapped nervously around the hallway. But it was no use. She'd have to think of something else.

According to the Grimlet twins, the typical kitchen was well stocked with the type of common household items—like baking powder, seltzer water, furniture polish, frozen peas, and so forth—that could be combined to produce the most marvelous explosive messes. Jane hoped that some of the Grimlets' criminal mastermindfulness had rubbed off on her, and that she'd be able to figure out how to create something powerful enough to blast through the locked front door.

This was not the most reasonable or realistic thought Jane had ever had. Even if she'd found piles and piles of common household items, she wouldn't have had the slightest idea what to do with them. But as it turned out, this wasn't important. When she got to Captain Rojo Herring's kitchen, all she found were stacks of empty jelly jars, half a loaf of toast, and a truly horrible smell.

"Gah!" Jane gagged. For a moment, she thought maybe the pirates had come back and were stinking up the place again. But the stench was actually coming from an expired carton of milk that Captain Rojo Herring had left out on the counter. Jane gagged again and went to pour the stinking milk down the drain.

The carton was one of the ones Lucinda Wilhelmina Hinojosa had been handing out, and Jane couldn't resist taking a quick peek at the picture of Ysquibel on the back. She hadn't paid much attention to the blurry photo before, but now she wanted to see what Captain Rojo Herring's friend looked like. Much to her surprise, he looked an awful lot like Captain Rojo Herring. In fact, Ysquibel and Captain Rojo Herring had faces that were as similar to each other as those of Melissa and Eddie Grimlet.

"Surely they're not twins . . ." Jane said. None of the articles she read in the birdcage mentioned anything about Ysquibel having a twin, and she didn't remember Captain Rojo Herring mentioning one either.

Now, there are people who claim that suddenly

having a wonderful insight is a lot like being hit by a thunderbolt, despite the fact that getting hit by an actual thunderbolt would not be wonderful at all. But in the next moment, this expression turned out to be more literally true for Jane than it had ever been for anyone else.

Lightning struck the creaky weather vane on the roof of the Mansion at the Top of Remarkable Hill. The crack of thunder deafened Jane as the hairs on the back of her neck bristled with electricity. And as her ears rang and her skin tingled, Jane realized that Ysquibel and Captain Rojo Herring didn't just look alike, they weren't twins, and they'd never been friends.

Captain Rojo Herring and Ysquibel were the same person!

After the Storm

The storm cleared off as quickly as it had started—almost as if someone had flipped a switch to turn it off. By the time dawn finished breaking, the new day was shaping up so delightfully that it seemed as if it were trying to make up for the unpleasantries of the night before. The air was filled with sunshine and with that wonderful wet smell that comes after a rain. It was also filled with thousands and thousands of butterflies.

They swirled and flitted silently through Remarkable. Rare Panamint swallowtails fluttered with common whirlabout skippers in the rosebushes in front of Filbert's Fine Grocery Store, while a flock of long dashes hovered around the geraniums in Mrs. Peabody's windows. There were many-spotted skipperlings spinning around an ornamental lamppost, confused cloudywings pirouetting in the trees in the park, and a herd of spangled fritillaries flitting over the waters of Lake Remarkable.

It was a marvel to behold, unless you happened to be Dr. Bayonet—in which case it an unspeakable nightmare.

"Nooooo! Ahhhhhh! Nooooo!" he shouted as he chased after the butterflies with a small lepidopterologist's net. Several glass panes in his butterfly domes had shattered during the storm, and every last one of his specimens had escaped. "Come back! Come back! Oh, please come back!"

But the butterflies didn't come back. In fact, they were acting very much as if they didn't want to be recaptured at all. And Dr. Bayonet—who had spent the last few years catering to their every need—was starting to feel unappreciated. A great purple hairstreak fluttered past him, and he swung at it and missed. In the process, he smacked himself in the shin.

"Owwwww!" he yelled. "Stupid butterflies! Stupid

hobby!" Dr. Bayonet threw his net on the ground and jumped up and down on it until it was broken into twelve pieces.

But this outburst of temper didn't make him feel any better—and the butterflies continued to fly away without a care in the world. It was as if they were taunting him with their freedom.

Dr. Bayonet felt his temper surge again. As far as he was concerned, those ungrateful little insects could just go take care of themselves. Once they were forced to find their own food, maybe then they'd learn to appreciate the fresh fruit, sweet nectar, milkweed, and sugar water he brought to them every morning on a silver breakfast tray.

"I don't need you!" he screamed at the butterflies. "I have other things I can do with my life. I can go back to being a dentist! Just try to stop me!"

But, of course, the butterflies put no effort whatsoever into stopping him. Dr. Bayonet kicked the broken net into some shrubbery and turned to stride purposefully back to the office he'd abandoned nearly two years ago. Unfortunately, he didn't see Jane in his path until he'd nearly tripped over her.

"Watch out, you!" he snapped, which was quite

unfair, given that he was the one who hadn't been paying attention to where he was going.

"Sorry, Dr. Bayonet," Jane said. She was tired and bedraggled from spending half the night in a birdcage, and the other half searching for Captain Rojo Herring in the storm. "I was just looking for my friend. You haven't seen anyone around here who's dressed like a pirate, have you?"

"Of course I haven't. What a ridiculous question. Now move! I have to get back to work!"

Dr. Bayonet shoved Jane out of the way as he marched down the hill toward town, and Jane returned to looking for Captain Rojo Herring and the pirate crew.

"They have to be here somewhere!" she tried to reassure herself as she scanned the lake's surface. "The storm must have slowed them down." Deep down, however, she was starting to believe she was too late.

Then she saw something that made her heart drop to her stomach. It was *The Mozart Kugeln*, and it was crumpled up in a sad little heap at the edge of the lake. Although *The Mozart Kugeln* had been a yar little vessel in its day, the storm had been too much for it. The yawl had been torn from stem to stern. Her masts were bent and her sails were ripped to ribbons.

Jane remembered what Captain Rojo Herring had told her about not being able to swim, and she began to worry that something truly terrible had happened to him. She wasn't sure what she should do. Should she summon the fire department, scream for help, or just keep looking?

"Jane?"

Jane nearly jumped out of her skin at the sound of her name. She turned to see that it was her grandfather who'd called to her, and she ran over to him as fast as her legs would carry her.

"You're okay!" Grandpa John said. "Oh, thank goodness. Penelope Hope said you didn't come home last night. I've been looking for you everywhere. Your father's out looking, too. He was frantic when he realized you were out in that storm."

"He was?"

"Of course he was—and he's been much too scared to tell your mother that he'd lost you, but that doesn't matter now. You're not missing anymore."

"And you're not in jail anymore!" she said, hugging

him hard. She'd never been so happy to see anyone in her life.

"I'm not," Grandpa agreed.

"But how did you get out? Did the Grimlet twins help you escape?"

"No, no. Nothing as exciting as that. Detective Burton Sly let me go this morning. Apparently they've got bigger problems with the bell tower now than some missing ropes—and it seems they needed space in the jail for three rather smelly pirates they captured last night."

"Was Captain Rojo Herring with them? Those three pirates kidnapped him! It was horrible!"

"That would be horrible," Grandpa said. A great spangled fritillary landed on his head, and he shooed it away. "But I think it's okay now. He must have gotten away from them. They were complaining bitterly that their captain had escaped their clutches again, and they were insisting that the town was going to owe them a new captain if he got away while they were being held in jail."

Jane was so relieved her legs went wobbly. Captain Rojo Herring was all right! He hadn't drowned, and he wouldn't be hauled back to life at sea after all.

"But, Grandpa, did you know he's not really a pirate captain! It turns out he's really Ysquibel, the missing musician."

"I had my suspicions," Grandpa said, but Jane barely paid attention to him. Instead, she told him all about her night in the birdcage, and how she'd managed to figure out his real identity. Then she told him all about how she managed to escape the Mansion at the Top of Remarkable Hill by sliding down the gangplank during the storm, and how she tracked the pirates to the lake by following their boot prints in the mud.

"Just think, once I tell everyone who Captain Rojo Herring really is, I'll be famous!" Jane said happily "The members of S.Y.N!C. will probably give me a medal. I might even get my picture in the paper. Maybe it'll turn out that I'm really good at finding lost people. Maybe Detective Burton Sly will consult with me on all his missing person cases."

"Hmph," Grandpa John said quietly. The great spangled fritillary drifted back over to him and then settled on his hand. He moved the butterfly up to his face so he could examine its bright orange wings more closely.

"Did you hear me, Grandpa? I bet even Grandmama will be impressed with me. It's big news, isn't it?"

"It's big news indeed," Grandpa said. The butterfly climbed on his fingers for a moment, and then it flew away.

"Funny thing about these butterflies. Do you think anyone would care much about them if they weren't so beautiful?"

"I don't know," Jane said impatiently. She didn't want to talk about butterflies. She wanted to talk about finding Ysquibel.

"But if they weren't beautiful, then collectors wouldn't kill them and mount them on display boards with pins so that they can look at them any time they want."

"Not all collectors are like that. Dr. Bayonet doesn't kill his butterflies. He keeps them safe so that people can appreciate them. And I'm sure the butterflies love his sanctuary."

"You think?" Grandpa asked. "If they love it so much, then why did they all fly away when they got the chance?"

Jane did not have a good answer for this. She stared at the throngs of butterflies skimming over the surface of the lake, flitting among the blackberry bushes on the shore, and whirling in the air as if they could not get enough of the fresh air and sunshine.

"Maybe they just wanted to do something else for a while," Jane said finally, but she wasn't sure she was right.

"Maybe they've wanted to do something else for their whole lives. The world is a wonderfully rich place, especially when you aren't trapped by thinking that you're only as worthwhile as your best attribute."

Grandpa pulled a packet of figgy doodles out of his pocket and threw one into the lake. The cookie sank like a fruit-filled rock. Then Jane saw just the faintest ripple in the water—as if something had swum over to eat it.

"It's the problem with Remarkable, you know," Grandpa said. "Everyone is so busy being talented, or special, or gifted, or wonderful at something that sometimes they forget to be happy. Does Ysquibel seem happy to you?"

Jane thought about it for a moment. "Well, sure. I guess so."

"Do you think he'll stay happy once you tell everyone who he really is?"

"No. I guess he won't."

"Then maybe you should think about keeping his secret."

Jane swallowed hard. The visions she had of being famous for finding Ysquibel disappeared like storm clouds in a Remarkable sky.

Grandpa flicked another figgy doodle into the lake. Jane watched the water ripple again ever so slightly.

"Grandpa? Is that . . . ?"

Grandpa smiled at her.

"That, my dear, is my secret. And she's been my secret for a long time. You'll help me keep it, won't you?"

Jane nodded. Grandpa handed her a figgy doodle of her own, and she tossed it out into the water. There was a flash of dark turquoise, and the cookie disappeared. It was so quick that Jane couldn't truly be sure she'd seen anything at all.

At the Dentist's Office

While Jane and Grandpa fed figgy doodles to Lucky, Grandmama Julietta Augustina was surveying the wreckage of the bell tower. It was hard to believe that only yesterday it had stood so proudly in the middle of town. Now it was just a pile of twisted metal, crushed cement, and splintered wood.

"And we never even got to hear its song," Taftly Wocheywhoski said. The tower's fifty-seven bells were dented and scattered across the post office lawn. He was surprised to find that there were tears in his eyes.

Angelina Mona Linda Doe was also on the verge of weeping. Her masterpiece—the crown jewel of all her architectural achievements—was gone forever. All of those months of planning and scheduling—all of those pie charts, graphs, lists, and spreadsheets—had been for nothing.

"I don't understand," she said. "The tower was structurally sound enough to withstand that storm. Only something incredibly powerful could have knocked it over."

"Maybe lightning struck it?" Grandmama said.

"Lightning couldn't have caused this much damage. It looks like it was hit by a bulldozer."

"Maybe it was. Maybe that crazy old man who stole the ropes yesterday came back during the storm and bulldozed it while no one was around," Taftly Wocheywhoski said.

"Don't be ridiculous," Grandmama told him. "That's my husband you're talking about."

"You're married?"

"Of course. I've been married for years and years. You know that."

"And your husband is a crazy bulldozer driver?"

"I thought I told you to stop being ridiculous. My husband is not even remotely crazy, and furthermore, he had nothing to do with this."

"How can you be so sure?" Taftly Wocheywhoski demanded.

"Because my husband spent last night in jail. And besides, Detective Burton Sly took three suspects into custody this morning. Isn't that right, detective?"

Detective Burton Sly had been crawling around on the ground with a magnifying glass, looking for clues in the bell tower's destruction. He stood to join the conversation.

"That's correct, Madam Mayor. One of my junior detectives spotted three men fleeing from the scene shortly after the bell tower was wrecked. The men were apprehended, identified as pirates, and taken to jail for questioning."

"You see, Taftly? Pirates did it. Not my husband."

"Ahem," Detective Burton Sly said as he shook his head. "Madam Mayor, as much as it pains me to contradict you, I don't think those pirates are the culprits. They had neither the strength nor the cunning to wreak this kind of havoc."

"Aha!" Taftly Wocheywhoski said. "So it was that crazy old bulldozer driver."

Detective Burton Sly shook his head once more.

"No. It was someone else entirely. Or should I say, something else entirely. Observe."

He pointed to the ground. Grandmama, Taftly Wocheywhoski, and Angelina Mona Linda Doe gasped. There, in the mud, was a series of giant, three-toed footprints leading from the wreckage of the bell tower down to the lakeshore. They were the kind of footprints that could only have been made by a largish cryptozoological creature, and they were the first sign in a long time that Lucky was alive and well in Lake Remarkable.

"Well, well, well," Grandmama Julietta Augustina said. "Would you look at that." She turned back to Detective Burton Sly. "I need you to assemble a team of your finest junior detectives. I want them to document and collect every shred of evidence at this scene. I want to send the Scottish Parliament irrefutable proof that a large and particularly elusive lake monster lives here."

"Madam Mayor, for such an important endeavor, perhaps it would be best if I collected the evidence myself."

"I appreciate the offer, but I'm afraid I have another assignment for you, and it's simply much too important to trust to a lesser detective."

Detective Burton Sly nodded. "I'm at your service,

Madam Mayor. Just tell me what it is you want me to do."

Meanwhile, Dr. Bayonet arrived at his office. It had been a long time since he'd set foot in it—a very long time—but nonetheless, he was surprised to discover that he hardly recognized his own waiting room. He could have sworn he'd hung framed pictures of butterflies on the wall, but now they seemed to have been replaced by posters which decried the evils of poor oral health. He didn't remember leaving all of those packed moving boxes in the corner either. Then he noticed a series of wet circles leading through the waiting room into the exam room. Someone had broken in! And that someone had been walking around on stilts.

Alarmed, he opened the exam room door and looked inside. There he saw a wet and unkempt pirate sleeping soundly in his dental chair—a dental chair that he was sure had been covered in red upholstery, not blue.

"What is the meaning of this?" Dr. Bayonet bellowed. "Who are you?" The bedraggled-looking fellow jumped to his feet—or rather, to his peg legs.

"I am Captain Rojo Herring," the startled man replied.

"Why are you sleeping in my exam room?"

"Um . . ." Captain Rojo Herring said unhelpfully. "Um . . . I'm not exactly sure." He remembered being kidnapped. He remembered the fierce storm, and he even remembered closing his eyes as Lucky charged toward him, ready to tear him to pieces.

Only she hadn't. Instead of chomping him in her powerful jaw, she'd gently grabbed him by the scruff of his pirate jacket and carried him up to the surface. Next thing Captain Rojo Herring knew, he was being dropped on solid ground some distance away from the lake. He scrambled to his feet just in time to see Lucky lurch wildly away. Moments later, he'd heard the horrible sound of splitting wood and clanging metal—just as if a structure holding fifty-seven bells had been smashed to smithereens by a large cryptozoological creature with a powerful tail—which, incidentally, was exactly what had happened.

"I'm still waiting for an explanation," Dr. Bayonet said sternly. But Captain Rojo Herring still didn't have one. His memories of what happened after he was rescued from the lake were hazy and strange. Maybe he'd banged his head when Lucky dropped him on the shore. Maybe he'd just accidentally drunk too much lake water. He'd heard the shouts of his pirate crew as they started to search for him. He knew they would find him soon if he didn't get moving.

As he staggered away from Jeb, Ebb, and Flotsam, Captain Rojo Herring found himself drawn toward the dentist's office. It was almost as if destiny—or something larger than destiny—was guiding him there. The door was unlocked when he arrived, and the office was quiet and dry. As he made himself comfortable in the dentist's chair, he was overcome with the feeling that for the first time ever, he was exactly where he was supposed to be. It was a very strong impression, and a very nice one, too. It was also, oddly enough, not so different than the wonderful sensation he'd had when he first laid eyes on his mystery woman.

Of course, by the cool light of day, it all seemed a bit dramatic and ridiculous. Had he really believed fate had guided him to a dentist's office? Why on earth would fate do such a thing?

"I'm afraid I have made some sort of a mistake,

Dr. Pike," he told Dr. Bayonet. "I do hope you'll pardon the intrusion."

"Dr. Pike? Who the devil is Dr. Pike?"

"I assumed you were. That's what the name says on your office door."

Dr. Bayonet turned and looked. The pirate was right. His door did say Dr. Pike on it.

"Someone is playing tricks on me," Dr. Bayonet said crossly. Then the door opened, and much to Dr. Bayonet's amazement, another dentist walked in.

"Ah," the mystery dentist said. "You must be from the moving company. I wasn't expecting you so early after that storm last night."

"Moving company?" Dr. Bayonet said. "What are you talking about? Who are you?"

"I'm Dr. Pike. This is my dental office."

"No it isn't! It's where I work," Dr. Bayonet told her, sounding even more cross. It had been a very trying day.

"I assure you, this has been my dental office for two years. But if you feel strongly about working here, I suppose you can have it. I'm leaving for a new job anyway."

"No!" screeched Captain Rojo Herring. "No! No! No! No! No!" Both dentists turned to stare at him.

"You can't leave!" Captain Rojo Herring tried to explain. "I came here to find you! That's what destiny was trying to tell me." His mouth widened into a loopy smile of love.

Dr. Pike smiled back—but her smile was a smile of professional glee, not love. All of the generic jelly from Munch that Captain Rojo Herring had eaten had done terrible things to his enamel and his gums—and she was now looking at the most beautiful set of rotten teeth she'd seen in a long, long time.

The Return of the Captain

Detective Burton Sly was on a mission. It was the mission that the mayor had entrusted him with, and it was of the utmost importance.

"It would appear that the Grimlet twins have developed a real working weather machine," Grandmama had told Detective Burton Sly before sending him on his way. She was a little impressed, despite herself. "Of course, they can't be allowed to keep it. Think of the trouble they'll cause."

"Yes, ma'am," Detective Burton Sly said. He'd already prepared extensive dossiers on the Grimlet twins and had some pretty good ideas about where to look. "Do you want me to haul them off to jail when I find them? We can make room."

"Oh dear lord, no. They'd adore being arrested. Anyway, there's no law against creating a storm."

"Yes, ma'am. I suppose you're right."

"And please inform them that they've won first place in the science fair. They've certainly earned it, and I can't think of anything they'd hate more."

It did not take Detective Burton Sly long to find the weather machine. He'd gotten some tips, followed a few leads, and then finally tracked the Grimlet twins' movements up Mount Magnificent to the most secluded spot in all of Remarkable. He'd expected that he'd find the Grimlet twins with their invention, but they were nowhere to be seen. Instead, he found Ms. Schnabel. She was sitting on the muddy ground in a clearing and staring at the weather machine with a look of great sadness and longing.

"I suppose yer 'ere to claim this 'ere weather machine for Mayor Doe," she said. She hadn't looked up when Detective Burton Sly arrived. Until she spoke, he wasn't sure if she knew he was there.

"Yes, ma'am. She asked me to make sure it was not in the possession of the Grimlet twins."

"Aye, makes sense, that does. But I've already done 'alf yer job for ye. I be the one who turned it off and chased those scurvy Grimlet twins back to their house. Little buggers would a kept that storm going all week if I 'adn't."

Detective Burton Sly stepped forward to examine the weather machine. It was bigger than a breadbox, smaller than a convection oven, and had a complex control panel comprised of barometers, thermostats, hygrometers, and anemometers. It was hard to believe that something so small could have wreaked so much havoc.

"I can see I'll need to keep a closer eye on those Grimlet twins," he said.

Ms. Schnabel snorted. "And good luck to ye wiv that."

"This is, of course, bad news for me since I recently discovered that Remarkable is home to one of the most notorious lawbreakers in the world. I'll have to keep my eye on her as well."

"Wot's that supposed to mean?" Ms. Schnabel demanded, but the detective did not answer her. He was attempting to pick up the weather machine, but he underestimated its weight and pulled several muscles.

"My back!" he cried as he staggered around the clearing. "I think I've thrown my back out!" He collapsed on the ground, twitching with pain.

"I could o' told ye it was heavy," Ms. Schnabel said unhelpfully.

"But you're rather strong, aren't you? Perhaps you could assist me in taking it back to town?"

"That all depends," Ms. Schnabel said. "Wot's the mayor plannin' on doing wiv it when you gets it to 'er?"

"I suspect she'll destroy it. We certainly don't want anyone tinkering with our weather again."

"Aye, but what a shame that be," Ms. Schnabel said, hoisting the weather machine onto her shoulder as if it weighed no more than a baby. "Seems like such a contraption could 'ave its uses."

"Yes, indeed," Detective Burton Sly said, wincing as he dragged himself back to his feet. "For example, I suspect it would be quite handy if one were interested in raising a ship from the bottom of the Sea of Cortez."

Ms. Schnabel stared at him, astonished. "Wot do ye know about the Sea of Cortez?"

"I think everyone knows of the fate of *The Wild Three O'Clock*, Captain Penzing."

Ms. Schnabel set the weather machine back down. Her astonishment transformed into amazement. "Ye knows who I am?"

"Of course I do. I am the world's greatest detective," Detective Burton Sly replied modestly. "Also, your sister was kind enough to confide in me."

"Gar! She has a mouth bigger than Moby Dick."

"I can assure you that I would have figured it out even without her help. I'd already learned that there is no such person as Ms. Delilah Schnabel. And more importantly, I learned that the person who was living under the name of Ms. Delilah Schnabel arrived in town and started working as a teacher at the public school seven years ago. And it was roughly nine years ago that a certain Mad Captain Penzing was released from prison and into the custody of her family."

"Aye. It took me two years to earn me teaching certificate before Mayor Doe could offer me the job. I be indebted to her for giving me the chance to try to start a new life—the kind of life that me parents might take some pride in. But respectable citizenry seems to be beyond me sometimes . . ."

"Then why don't you return to the sea?"

Ms. Schnabel sighed. "Because I made a promise to me parents not to go back to pirating. It was in exchange for getting busted out of the brig, but now I can see that the brig would be preferable to the life I've chosen."

"Interesting," Detective Burton Sly said. "I was not aware that your parents were pirates."

"Har. That'll be the sunny day," Ms. Schnabel said. "They wouldn't be caught dead having anything to do with piracy."

"Perhaps I've been misinformed, then," Detective Burton Sly said. "My understanding was that pirates only have to keep promises they make to other pirates."

"Aye," Ms. Schnabel said. "That be part of the Pirates' Code."

"Then I guess I don't see what's stopping you from going off to lead the life you love. Surely not a promise made to a bunch of landlubbers."

Ms. Schnabel gave Detective Burton Sly a suspicious stare. "How is it a great detective like yerself seems so invested in getting me to return to me life of crime?"

"Ma'am, without great lawbreakers, there would be no need for great detectives."

Ms. Schnabel sighed and stepped away from the weather machine. "Ye might as well let the mayor destroy it," she said sorrowfully. "As much as I'd like to hightail it back to me life at sea, a captain ain't worth much without a crew."

"I could see how that might pose a problem. But as it so happens, I might have a solution for you. And it is a solution that helps me rid Remarkable of three troublemakers who have no appreciation whatsoever for great detective work."

He was thinking of Ebb, Jeb, and Flotsam, of course. He told her where to find them, and even lent her the money for their bail. By the next day, Mad Captain Penzing the Horrific, the weather machine, and her new pirate crew had disappeared.

After the Aftermath

A town like Remarkable only has happy endings. The big storm might have seemed like a disaster, but actually, it left many good things in its fearsome wake. With the bell tower gone, Lucky was now safe—which made Grandpa very happy. Mrs. Peabody was happy, because the town was now almost entirely free of pirates. She decided she didn't mind Captain Rojo Herring so much because he was such a good customer and was also so polite.

Lucinda Wihelmina Hinojosa was happy, because while she was trapped under the bandstand during the storm, she'd met Johnny November, the band's drummer, and had fallen in love with his perfect sense of rhythm. And if Johnny November didn't share her passion for locating Ysquibel, he never let her know.

This didn't exactly make Anderson Brigby Bright happy, but at least he gave up trying to impress her with his singing, which made everybody else in town ecstatic. He'd decided to be in love with Anastasia Elise Ellenton instead, who was a champion roller skater. Anderson Brigby Bright was as terrible at roller-skating as he was a singing, but at least with this new hobby, he was only hurting himself.

Grandmama Julietta Augustina was perhaps the happiest of all. Not only had Lucky's brief foray out of the lake given her the evidence she needed to prove to the Scottish Parliament that Lucky was the superior lake monster, but she'd also learned that Dr. Pike had decided to stay on as Remarkable's dentist, which meant she got to call Mayor Kate Chu and give her the bad news.

"It's just how things worked out," Grandmama said into the phone in a voice dripping with false sympathy. "Better luck next time and all that."

The reason that Dr. Pike had decided to stay was because of Captain Rojo Herring. "There's a year's worth of tricky dentistry in that mouth," she said dreamily, staring at his receding gums. Captain Rojo Herring looked dreamy, too—but that's because he was in love with Dr. Pike and not really thinking about the extractions, root canals, implantations, and cleanings he was about to face.

Of course, the reason that Captain Rojo Herring had decided to stay was because he thought his secret was safe. And the reason he thought his secret was safe was because Jane decided not to reveal his true identity. Normally, she might have taken some pride in this fact, and might have even enjoyed knowing that some of the lovely things that were happening in town were because of her. But Jane was too sick to feel much of anything beside feverish and sneezy. She'd caught a miserable, horrible cold as a result of spending the night in the drafty mansion.

For the next week and a half, Jane stayed in her room, going downstairs only to make herself soup and tea when the rest of her family forgot to bring her any. Grandpa John came over a few times with figgy doodles and told her all about his long and secret friendship with Lucky, and Grandmama Julietta Augustina sent Stilton over with an extra-big box of Kleenex.

Jane pulled out a tissue, blew her nose, and then got back into bed so that she could watch a TV show about dog grooming. But as she was getting settled under her covers, the most extraordinary thing happened. A large rock hit her bedroom window and shattered it into a million pieces.

"I told you that rock was too big!" came Eddie Grimlet's voice from outside.

"And I told you not to throw it so hard," Melissa yelled back at him. There was a scuffling sound, and Jane knew that they had started one of their kicking fights.

She dragged herself out of bed and looked through the new hole in her window.

"Achoo!" she sneezed pitifully. Eddie and Melissa stopped fighting long enough to grin wickedly at her.

"Jane! Jane! You have to come with us right away!"

"I can't," Jane sniffed. "I'm sick."

"Who cares," Eddie said. "A package is coming for you today down at the post office!"

"A package? For me?" Jane found this so implausible that she immediately suspected the Grimlet twins were trying to play some kind of a trick on her. "No one ever sends me mail. And even if someone did, how would you know about it?"

"Dearest Jane," Melissa said, "we make it our business to know all kinds of things we're not supposed to know. But that's not what's important. What's important is that the package is from Mad Captain Penzing the Horrific."

Mad Captain Penzing the Horrific. Jane had told the Grimlet twins about Ms. Schnabel's real identity right after she left town. Eddie swore he'd suspected it all along, and Melissa claimed that it was obvious to anyone paying attention, but Jane could tell that they were both as astonished by the news as she was.

"But why would Ms. Schnabel—I mean Mad Captain Penzing the Horrific—send me a package?" Jane wondered.

"That's what we thought," Eddie replied. "I mean, she barely even noticed you. We think the package must actually be for us."

"We think she's decided to send back our weather machine," Melissa explained.

Jane was too tired to care if they got their weather machine back, but the Grimlet twins would not be ignored.

"We offered to sign for it after it arrived," Melissa told her, "but for some reason, the postal employees didn't trust us to bring it to you."

"So we need you to come," Eddie said. "We'd prefer it if you came quietly, but if you won't, well, we have our methods."

"Oh, fine," Jane grumbled as she went to get dressed.

Three minutes later, she was walking to town with the Grimlet twins. Even though her nose was dripping and she was feeling light-headed, Jane knew that she should enjoy her time with the twins while she could. She would not be seeing them nearly as much anymore. They had been unexpectedly re-enrolled at Remarkable's School for the Remarkably Gifted. The esteemed Dr. Presnelda had decided that it would be easier to reinstate them than to admit that public school kids had beaten her superior students at the science fair.

"How do you like being back at the gifted school?" Jane asked them.

"It's mind-numbingly horrendous," Melissa said as she tried to trip Eddie with a sharp stick. "Worse than I remember."

"Dismally abysmal," Eddie complained as he grabbed the stick away from Melissa and tried to poke her in the eye with it. "But don't worry. We're planning on getting expelled again soon. It'll be harder this time, but we have a few ideas that are much, much worse than the blue bomb."

Jane decided she didn't mind if it took them a while to figure it out. Having a life that was quite ordinary didn't seem so bad anymore.

When they arrived at the once-again plain post office, Jane sat down with the Grimlet twins on the bench outside to wait for her package to be delivered. Eddie and Melissa pulled out a large stash of straws and began shooting wrappers at everyone who walked past.

It was a remarkably fine day again, as it would continue to be, since the Grimlet twins had lost possession of their weather machine. In the distance, Jane could see Dr. Bayonet crashing through the bushes with his butterfly net. Once he'd calmed down, he decided he'd rather rebuild his butterfly sanctuary than return to dentistry. Dr. Bayonet ran past Grandpa John, who was walking to Lake Remarkable with a fresh packet of figgy doodles.

An hour went by with no sign of any deliveries. Then, just as Jane was starting to think that she wasn't getting a package after all, a big mail truck pulled to a stop in front of the post office, and a mailman unloaded a plain brown medium-sized box.

"It's too small for the weather machine," Melissa said glumly.

"And the weather machine wouldn't need air holes," Eddie said. They could see that someone had punched small openings in the top of the box in the shape of a skull and crossbones.

"One of you kids named Jane Doe?" the mailman asked.

"That's me," Jane said.

"Sign here."

Jane signed her name, and the mailman put the box at her feet. For a moment, Jane was almost afraid to open it. It was bound to contain something boring— like a sweater, or a puzzle with missing pieces, or maybe even some homework Ms. Schnabel had forgotten to give her before leaving town. Then all the fun of anticipating getting a truly exciting gift would be gone.

"You'd better hurry up," Eddie told her. "If you

320

keep us in suspense much longer, we're going to be inclined to steal that box and open it ourselves."

Melissa handed Jane a small dagger she kept hidden in her sock, and Jane used it to cut through the packing tape on the top of the plain brown medium-sized box. She lifted off the lid and looked inside. And inside, she saw the most marvelous plain brown medium-sized puppy. The puppy looked up and yawned at Jane sleepily as she reached in to pick him up.

He was a very ordinary dog—perhaps the plainest, most ordinary dog that ever lived.

"Oh," Jane said. "Oh, isn't he the most beautiful dog ever!"

Melissa raised a crooked eyebrow at her while Eddie dug around in the box and found a note from Ms. Schnabel.

"Hey," he said happily. "This note's addressed to me!"

"It's addressed to both of us," Melissa said.

"Well, my name's first, so I'm probably supposed to read it first."

"Interesting, but wrong," Melissa said as she made a grab for the note in his hand. Eddie dodged her grasp, but she managed to get a hold of the back of his shirt. They scuffled over it for a good ten minutes until Melissa managed to pin Eddie to the ground with her foot and pry the note out of his fingers.

"Dear Melissa," the note read. "I'm going to assume that Jane is too busy with her new puppy to read this note, and that you managed to best Eddie in whatever battle the two of you got into. I'm gone and I won't be coming back. Being a pirate is so much more gratifying than teaching fifth graders (no offense). But on my travels, I discovered this puppy. Actually, he was on *The Wild Three O'Clock* for a whole week before I even noticed him. A pirate ship is no place for a dog, so I thought I'd send him to Jane, seeing as how Jane has always wanted a dog of her own.

Yours at sea,

Captain Penzing the Horrific.

P.S. The dog's name is Dirt.

P.P.S. The weather machine has been immensely helpful. Much more so than Ebb, Jeb, and Flotsam, who are the three most worthless pirates I've ever met, excluding the three of you.

P.P.P.S. I am NEVER EVER giving the weather machine back, so there."

"The nerve of her," Eddie said self-righteously.

"Treating other people's property with such a lack of respect." Melissa ripped Captain Penzing's note into shreds and scattered the pieces across the post office lawn. Then the Grimlet twins fixed their attention on Dirt, who was wriggling in Jane's arms and giving her excited puppy kisses.

"He's not so bad," Melissa said. "For such a plain dog."

"I suspect he might even be useful," Eddie added. "Useful to us, I mean."

Jane was too busy with her new puppy to notice that they were talking to her. The Grimlet twins weren't used to having Jane ignore them, and they didn't like it one bit.

"You know, Jane," Eddie said loudly. "There are a lot of crime-fighting dogs in the world. But I've never heard of a crime-causing dog. If you let us work with him, we could turn him into the world's first canine criminal mastermind."

"He could break into people's homes and destroy their rugs, pee on their slippers, and steal their news-papers. Or we could teach him to chase cats up trees so that firemen would have get their ladders out to rescue them," Melissa suggested. "Let's go to our house and start making plans. You can come over, Jane. We'll have snacks, and we'll even let you see our secret lair if you want to."

"No, thanks," Jane said, looking up from her puppy for the first time since she'd gotten him. Her face was a happy mix of amazement and joy.

"What do you mean?" Melissa demanded. She had never in a million years guessed that Jane wouldn't accept an invitation to enter their creepy black house. "We're giving Dirt a chance to be something special, you know."

"He doesn't need to be special," Jane said firmly. "All he needs to be is my dog." And with that, she walked home with Dirt cuddled in her arms.

And so Dirt Doe became the newest member of the Doe household. "Perhaps Jane will become a great dog trainer!" her father said as he watched his middle daughter walk Dirt in the backyard on a leash. Her mother nodded enthusiastically. "Yes. I think she's found her special skill at last!"

This proved not to be the case, although it was not necessarily Jane's fault. Dirt wasn't the kind of dog who paid much attention to dog training. He only did what he was told occasionally, and that was only if Jane was offering him a dog treat at the time. He liked to bark loudly early in the morning, had a minimal interest in going outside to use the bathroom, and a maximal enthusiasm for chewing up shoes, paintbrushes, and scientific calculators. He also liked to dig up the flower garden and steal food from the table.

Grandmama Julietta Augustina quickly developed a soft spot for Dirt. When Mad Captain Penzing the Horrific left town, Salzburg decided to go with her. Grandmama wasn't willing to admit how much she missed the parrot, but she did find that Jane's dog helped fill the parrot-sized hole that Salzburg had left in her life. She often took Dirt for walks when Jane was busy at school and had been known, from time to time, to take him to the mayor's office with her.

"Not much of a dog if you ask me," Grandmama said fondly as she watched him knock over one of Anderson Brigby Bright's paint cans and track photorealistic green footprints all over the living room rug.

Jane didn't mind Grandmama's words, because Dirt was the most amazing thing that had ever happened to her—and unremarkably, Jane and Dirt became the best of friends.

ACKNOWLEDGMENTS

Like many writers, I am deeply insecure and I would undoubtedly still be writing and rewriting the first chapter of this book if not for the encouragement of many fine people.

One of the finest is my agent, Faye Bender, who is not just a fantastic human being but is also so incredibly good at what she does. For her patience with my endless questions, her cheerful support, and her ability to arrange surprise cupcake deliveries, she has earned my undying devotion.

Then there is my equally wonderful editor, Nancy Conescu, who has been an enthusiastic advocate of this story, and whose keen eye and fabulous revision notes have made *Remarkable* so much more than it was when she first saw it. Additionally, I'd like to send a big thank you to the people at Dial/Penguin for making me feel so welcome as one of their new authors. In particular, I'd like to thank Andrew Harwell, Lauri Hornik, Rosanne Lauer, and Don Weisberg.

I'd be remiss if I didn't thank Meg Mitchell Moore, who did a lot of hand-holding during the querying and submission process, and her agent, Elisabeth Weed, who very kindly introduced me to Faye.

I also owe a huge debt of gratitude to my beloved writing groups. From the Cambridge Center of Adult Education's Zen Writing Group, I want to think Brina Cohen, Celia Judge, Dorothy Irving, Rick Stafford, Margaret Gooch, and Mordena Babich—who were there when *Remarkable* was started. And from my Santa Fe writing group, many thanks to Debra Auten, Hope Cahill, Janie Chodosh, Catherine Coulter, Jenny Owings Dewey, Nadine Donovan, Ana June, Karen Kraemer, Barbara Mayfield, and Lyn Searfoss, who gave me the encouragement, support, and suggestions I needed to finish it. Additionally, I'd like to thank my fellow Apocalypsies (an online group of debut novelists), for helping me find my way through revisions, copyedits, cover art, and release dates.

Margaret Foley and Jon Wilkins deserve special thanks for proofreading and commenting on several drafts of *Remarkable* (sometimes on very short notice over holiday weekends) before it went out into the world. And I'd like to thank Jon again, for years of support and faith in my writing. I also owe a thank you to Dash Foley-Wilkins, for his patience and for his many, many story suggestions (particularly those pertaining to pirates).

And finally, I'd like to thank my dogs, who made sure my writing days were never lonely (or particularly quiet or chaos-free). Robbie, Sandy, Matthew, and Luke—you are very good dogs. Oh-yes-you-are-good-dogs-oh-yes-you-are.